A Last Gift

Beca Lewis

Perception Publishing

ISBN-13: 978-1-7357843-5-9

Contents

One

I t came in the mail. How long it had sat in the mailbox Rhoberta Bree Mann—known as Bree—didn't know. It had been at least a month since she had put a foot outside her door, let alone checked her mail.

She only got the letter because the mailman, frustrated with the filled-to-overflowing mailbox, had dumped all her mail into a box, pounded on the door, and rang the doorbell before stomping away. Anger still poured out of him as he stepped into his truck. Bree was sure he would have slammed the truck door if it had one.

Before driving away, the mailman looked back at the house, and when he glimpsed Bree's face peeking from behind the curtain, pointed at the door, looking as stern as she had ever seen him. But after pulling away, he stopped and looked back at the house. He sighed, his lined face drooping. Bree almost felt sorry for him. He had been their mailman for many years, and he knew why she had not collected the mail.

Bree tried to find the energy to at least lift a finger to wave, but she couldn't. Instead, as he drove silently away, heading to the next house almost a quarter of a mile away, Bree gathered all the energy

1

she had, opened the door, and slid the box inside. She turned and shut the door with her back, allowing herself to slide to the floor and stare at the box in front of her.

It was dusty and falling apart at the seams. Did he find the box by the side of the road and decide it was a good way to get rid of the mail that had been collecting in her mailbox? The box looked like she felt. Old and abandoned.

How was she to know that inside the box of mail was her husband's last gift to her? Would it have made any difference? Days later, holding his letter in her hand, she would force herself to open it, dreading what it meant.

But that day, she closed her eyes, rolled over on her side, and lay on the floor. She could feel the draft on her back, the opening under the door that Paul had promised to fix but never got around to doing.

The memory of how frustrated she had been with him for not fixing it, how she had decided to do it herself but never had the chance, started the now-familiar wave of grief and guilt that fell on her like a blanket, and Bree wept again. Not caring that she was on the floor. Not caring that her nose was running, that she could smell herself, that her hair was full of tangles, and she couldn't remember the last time she had showered.

Not caring about anything at all. Except now, there was a box in front of her that demanded her attention. Bree knew that once she dealt with the box, it would open the door to living again. And that's not what she wanted.

Bree wanted her heart to stop beating. She wanted to join her husband wherever he was because she was sure he was waiting. He had promised. Long ago, on the day they married, he had promised that it wasn't just until death. It was forever.

But she couldn't even decide how to kill herself, let alone gather the courage to pull it off. The thought that someone would find her and have to deal with the mess added to her inability to leave this life.

She, who lived with everything in a neat order, everything in its place, could not force that terrible disorder on someone else. Drowning herself was an option. But that would mean driving to the lake and then finding a way to make herself stay underwater. Too hard to do.

That day, laying on the floor in her own mess, Bree didn't even have the courage to open her eyes, knowing that all she would see was disorder. A neglected house.

Under the table by the door, dirt screamed at her to get up. The unwashed dishes added their voice to the cacophony of voices in her head that told her she was a useless piece of work, had never deserved Paul, and it was her fault he had died.

But the box. The box was different. The voice of the box was both demanding and soothing. It was reminding Bree that, like it, she was still useful. The box aroused her curiosity, and that pissed her off. Because Bree knew that once she was curious, her time of mourning would come to a close. Life would move on. She would have to pretend to live instead of wanting to die.

So she lay there for another hour, finally sitting up, back still against the door, and stared at the box that called her to start living again. Sighing so hard it hurt her chest, she grabbed the box and dumped the mail onto the floor. Years of practice managing chaos and putting things in order kept her moving forward without thinking.

She made piles of junk mail, bills, the local papers, and the catalogs that she could never stop from arriving. She slid into a pile the cards she knew contained words of sympathy that would never change anything. She didn't want to see them.

But one letter stood out. Of course, Paul meant it to. Did he know she would be tempted to throw all the cards in the trash without opening them? Of course, he did.

Paul had taken no chances that she would ignore his letter. Stickers covered the envelope. Hearts, flowers, and tree stickers made the stamp barely visible in the corner.

Bree stared at the envelope addressed to her in handwriting as familiar as her own, and holding it close to her heart, she lay back down on the floor and asked the gods once more to "please, please, please, let me die."

Hours later, still alive and knowing death was not coming for her, she let herself drift back in time. Fingering the gold necklace with a tiny ruby in the center that he had given her as a wedding present, she remembered the moment she had first seen him, and turned to her friend and said, "I'm going to marry him."

Two

Thirty-one years in the past ...

Bree felt as if a hand had reached into her chest, squeezed her heart, and the words, "I'm going to marry him," came out of her mouth with no thinking on her part.

But once she said them, she knew they were true. A lifetime with this stranger stretched out before her, and she couldn't stop herself from laughing at the pure joy of that vision.

Almost as if he had heard her, the stranger she knew she would marry looked away from the group of people surrounding him, tilted his head, smiled at her, and then returned to the conversation.

The friend standing beside her laughed and said, "Yea, right. How's that going to happen? He's the most popular teacher here, and you're a lowly student."

"He teaches here?"

"What, you don't know who he is?"

"No."

"Then how do you expect to marry him?"

Tossing her head, causing her dark curls to bounce wildly, Bree answered, "I don't know. But I will. Wait and see."

Her friend laughed again. "Okay. But if you do—not saying that you will—I want to be your bridesmaid, since I was here when you first saw the love of your life."

"Deal, but only if you tell me everything you know about him."

"Are you serious?"

Bree turned to her friend. She had known Cindy Lee Jones since they were both six years old. Bree had turned from where she was hiding in the cloakroom on the first day of first grade, afraid to face the class, and saw a girl crouched behind the umbrella stand.

For a minute they stared at each other, not sure what to do. Finally, Bree gathered up the small amount of courage she had and asked, "Afraid to go out there?"

The girl, her blond hair streaming down her back, blue eyes brimming with tears, nodded yes.

"Me too. But if we're friends, we could go out together. I'm Bree."

It took a minute, but eventually, the girl answered, "Cindy."

Bree reached out her hand, Cindy stood, and they walked out together. The teacher took one look at the two of them, and to their great relief, put them side by side in the classroom. They had been side by side ever since.

Bree locked her hazel eyes into Cindy's blue ones and gave her a look. That look said it all. Cindy learned long ago that Bree didn't say things she didn't mean, and if she wanted something, she'd figure out a way to get it.

"Not here. At the coffee shop at the HUB."

Cindy looped her arm through Bree's, pulling her away, but Bree couldn't help herself. She stole one last look over her shoulder.

Although still talking to the gaggle of students, the man had moved so that he was watching her walk away. Bree turned around and smiled to herself. She knew he'd be watching.

Bree and Cindy spent the next hour huddled together at the campus coffee shop tucked inside a food court and recreation space called the HUB.

It was a good name for it. It was noisy with people coming and going, bright colors on the walls, and a tile floor that echoed sound mingled with the smell of coffee and food. But there were quiet corners if you wanted privacy.

Cindy found one of those corners, away from the hustle and bustle, while Bree paid for the drinks, figuring it was as good a bribe as any.

Once they settled in, Bree said she was ready to learn it all. Cindy laughed and told her everything she knew about the handsome and popular professor. It wasn't much. Mostly rumors about who he was and where he had come from. No one really knew. All Cindy knew for sure was that Paul Mann taught statistics, and even people who didn't like numbers tried to get into his class.

It wasn't just his tall Adonis good looks. It was the way he taught. The way he gathered people into interesting discussions. That's what Cindy had heard about him. But no matter how cool the statistics teacher was, Cindy wasn't interested. She was an artist. To her way of thinking, those two things didn't go together at all.

"Are you sure you want a man who thinks numbers are interesting?" Cindy asked her friend and waited for how Bree would rationalize this one.

Having grown up together, she knew Bree as well as anyone could. Bree shared, but only so much. On the other hand, Cindy was always spilling out her secrets to Bree. But to Bree's credit, she had used none of them against her or shared them with others.

However, Bree didn't realize that Cindy knew all of Bree's secrets. All of them. Even the ones Bree had kept from everyone. Cindy had made it her business to know them. It was a way to always protect her friend, even if Bree thought she didn't need it.

So as Bree asked about the man Bree said was her future husband, Cindy worried. Paul Stanford Mann looked a great deal like the boy who had broken Bree's heart. Not that Bree told her it was broken or even acted sad, but Cindy was sure it was there, buried under Bree's compulsion to get things done.

Cindy knew that Bree's heart was held together with her steely determination. Even though it had been Bree who had stretched out her hand in the coat closet, it was Cindy who kept the two of them together.

It was Cindy who made sure that Bree knew she always had a friend, even when Bree acted as if she didn't need one. Not believing her, Cindy had encouraged her to add more girls into their two-girl group until there were five of them. All different, but with one thing in common: to be more than their small town expected them to be.

They helped each other through school, supported each other's dreams, and when it was time to choose a college, all five of them decided to go together. So, even though a few of them planned to leave town as soon as they could, they went to the small community college in town instead, because that was the only place all of them got into. It meant two more years together before they went their separate ways.

And although Cindy knew they would all branch out into the world, they would stay in touch forever. They had made a pact in grade school and they would honor it. So even if Bree married Mr. Hunky professor, it wouldn't change anything.

Cindy was wrong, of course, but she believed it to be true that day in the coffee shop. So when two more members of their group wandered into the HUB looking for food, Cindy called them over, not fully appreciating how much everything would be different from then on.

Three

J udith Zoe took one look at Bree's face and then asked Cindy, "What's going on?"

"Bree just saw the man she's going to marry."

"Seriously?" April May Zane shrieked, plopping herself into a chair. She propped her chin on her hands and stared at the two of them, waiting for answers.

April's short curly light brown hair, deep brown eyes, and tiny body, combined with her happy-go-lucky nature, always reminded Cindy of a chipmunk. Especially when she was quivering with excitement, as she was at that moment.

Cindy shushed them both, saying, "Keep it down," and then laughed at their crestfallen looks.

April and Judith were so different that most people would never expect them to be friends, but it was their differences that kept them friends long after their last names brought them together.

Judith and April were the only two people in school whose last name started with a Z, so they were either always first or last in line in school. Usually, they were last in line, which gave them plenty of time to get to know each other.

They had met in second grade when April's family moved to town so her dad could teach at the community college.

Until then, Judith had stood alone in lines, wishing she had a friend. She was so lonely she thought she would die. Not that no one knew her, it was that everyone did, and then made fun of her. Not only because her last name started with a Z, but she was so much taller than everyone else.

Everywhere she went, she towered above all the other children. Only a few kids in sixth grade were taller than her. All the kids in elementary school saw her as a freak. Her flaming red hair didn't help. She was hard to miss. But no one wanted to be seen with her, which meant she was always alone.

Only Judith's size kept the kids from physically picking on her. And her temper. She had pushed one kid who kept taunting her, and that was enough to stop that kind of abuse. But it increased the unkind words and taunting, and she had been called into the principal's office to explain why she had done it. The unfairness of it all ate away at Judith's soul, and every day she felt more lonely and tortured.

And then, one day, there was someone else at the back of the line with her, someone who smiled at her and introduced herself as April May Zane. Judith had stared, not knowing what to say, having had no practice with friendly banter. She stuttered her name in return and then asked the obvious question before realizing it might be a sensitive one, and she may have ruined the friendship before it got started.

Instead, April had laughed and explained that her mother didn't know if she would be born in April or May. She just knew she'd be a girl. Felt it in her bones. But not knowing which month, she named her baby both April and May. It turned out she was born on May 2nd, but her parents had already decided that they liked the name April better.

"April showers bring May flowers," they would say when people asked about her two-month name. No one really understood what they meant, and April assumed they really didn't know either, but being parents in the seventies, fresh from living in a commune, it felt right to them.

Like her mother, April had a carefree, joyous nature, which balanced perfectly with Judith's solid common sense.

"Where's Marsha?" Bree asked, as April and Judith took seats across the table. "I don't feel like repeating this over and over again."

"Who knows?" Judith huffed.

Marsha Melinda Martin sometimes made Judith want to shake her, even though she secretly envied Marsha's ability to make her own decisions. Marsha was the one who was often missing, pursuing her personal agenda, never letting them know where she was, showing up when she felt like it.

Bree had met Marsha in dance class and invited her into their group without even checking with them. The four of them had been friends for a few years and didn't need anyone else. Then Marsha, whose parents had liked alliteration—as Marsha informed them that first day—trailed Bree to their lunch table and inserted herself into the group by latching onto Bree.

Judith thought that the best thing Marsha had going for her was her unbiased, unrelenting loyalty to Bree, which extended to the group because that was how Bree said it needed to be, and Marsha had agreed.

And Judith had to admit Marsha was loyal even when she was off doing her own thing. They could trust her with important things. But not about always being available. Everything was Marsha's timing, which meant no one wanted to wait for her to show up now to learn what was happening.

"Come on, tell us now," April begged, her brown eyes wide.

Bree hesitated, but before she could speak, Cindy hissed, "Well, Bree's future husband just walked in. But don't look!"

Cindy's "don't look" message was ignored. Both April and Judith turned in their chairs and then back to Bree and Cindy, but not before Paul saw them, turned red, and walked back out the door.

"Well, now you've done it," Cindy said.

Four

Paul turned to leave the room so quickly he bumped into a group of students trying to decide what to order, causing a minor flurry of "excuse mes" and appreciative looks from the women students and glares from the boys.

Outside in the hall, he leaned up against the wall, trying to get his breath even though the hall smelled of cleaning solution and body odor. He almost wished he hadn't taken that breath.

What was that about? He asked himself.

He was flustered and embarrassed over what? It was just a group of silly college girls sitting at a table staring at him. He was used to it. And it had been years since it had caused any reaction in him.

Why now? Paul thought he had long outgrown the response to his looks. He had never thought winning a genetic pool of good looks as something to be happy about. He would rather be invisible. As far as he was concerned, his looks were a problem, not a gift.

Growing up, he had been gangly and nerdy and mostly ignored by all his schoolmates. Now, as an adult, he knew he had been lucky in that respect. Instead of being ignored, he could have been bullied. Perhaps he had been—at least verbal bullying—but he hadn't noticed.

He had other things on his mind. More important things. Things he could never tell any of his schoolmates. They were secrets he would have to live with forever, and none of his schoolmates would ever understand, even if he wanted to tell them.

To take his mind off his problems, he decided to learn about the world around him. Even as a child, he experimented with possibilities. What would happen if he put an obstacle in an ant's path? The details and structure of life fascinated him, and everything else faded into the background.

Paul knew his parents worried about his lack of interest in other people or in having friends. But for him, his life was okay, and he was happy being invisible and left alone. School was easy. People were hard.

In high school, all that changed. He grew out of gangly. And the nerdy kid that no one had noticed became an object of tittering and long stares. Nothing had changed within him, but everything had changed about how the world saw him, and he began to live in a constant state of embarrassment at the looks he received and with a low-level terror that the boys who looked at him with hatred would physically turn on him.

One of his teachers, Mr. Drummond, noticing his discomfort, asked if Paul had studied any form of martial arts. He had not and wasn't interested. But Matthew Drummond spoke to Paul's parents, and they forced him to go to an Aikido class with Mr. Drummond, who loyally went to a beginner class with Paul, even though Matthew had been taking lessons for years.

Without Mr. Drummond accompanying him, Paul wouldn't have lasted the first thirty minutes. Or come back. Mr. Drummond dragged him to class twice a week until one day Paul realized the terror had faded.

By then, Mr. Drummond insisted Paul call him Matthew, or Mat, when they weren't in school. At first, Paul resisted. But after countless hours of practicing together, he found that having his teacher as a friend was the most important thing that had ever happened to him, and calling him by his first name felt okay. However, he could never bring himself to say Mat.

Paul learned quickly, and because of his diligent practice, Matthew was able to go back to his more advanced class, taking Paul with him. Matthew was the one Paul confided in about his embarrassment about girls. Matthew gave him tips on what to say, what to wear, and how to behave. He was the one who directed Paul to study statistics and astrophysics.

Without Matthew Drummond, Paul didn't know how he would have made it through high school or found the career that he loved so much.

Matthew Drummond had passed away a year ago, and his long lingering illness gave them time to deepen their friendship, knowing they had little time. As Matthew would say, "I have a lot to say, so listen up."

Not a day went by that Paul didn't miss Matthew, but today of all days, he wished he were there to help him understand why he was once again embarrassed after all these years. And afraid. And a little terrified. But he wasn't afraid of something that martial arts or statistics could fix.

The girl—the woman—who had walked into the room that morning was going to change his life. That, he knew without a doubt. It had already happened. His heart had leaped at the sight of her. An unbidden thought had come into his mind. How it could be possible, he didn't understand. It didn't follow his ordered view of the universe.

He had thought, "I'm going to marry her."

How? Why? He didn't know, but there it was, and what made it worse was he was pretty sure it was true. And that meant the life he had planned out for himself was probably over.

So when he saw her sitting there, and her friends had turned to look at him, he had fled.

Out in the hall, Paul breathed deeply, steadied himself, and decided to go home. He'd cancel office hours for the day. Heck, maybe even for the rest of the semester, so she would never walk into his office and make his heart slam against his ribs and lose his breath.

"Get a grip," he told himself. "This kind of thing doesn't happen."

Although Paul knew ghosts didn't exist, he knew life went on in some way, so he wasn't too surprised to hear Matthew's voice say, "And yet it does," because that was what Matthew would have said if he were still alive.

Paul also knew what Matthew would say next. "So, what are you going to do about it?"

His answer was, "I don't know."

Paul could almost see Matthew laughing his big laugh and feel the slap on his back, encouraging him not to get in the way of where the universe was going to take him.

Infinite possibilities in nature meant endless possibilities in life. That had been Matthew's motto and Paul tried to make it his, too. But it was not one he found easy to live. Instead, he would try to figure out what would happen before it did, always trying to plan the outcome.

Unlike Matthew, Paul was afraid of taking chances without studying every angle first. He knew all too well that sometimes things happen that change your life forever. And sometimes it is because of a stupid choice or a wrong action.

What terrified him this time was that it was possible that the outcome was already determined, and he had nothing to say about it.

Five

While all that was going on, the missing Marsha was in the library, her head buried in a book. She loved the library, where everything was quiet, peaceful, and orderly.

Marsha loved the feeling of holding a book in her hands and disappearing into another world, one of her own choosing. If she didn't like a book and the world it created, she could put it down and open another. Not like life.

Only when her stomach rumbled did she realize what time it was and that everyone was probably in the school's coffee shop having lunch together, wondering where she was.

Marsha could almost see the steam coming out of Judith's head at her absence. It gave her a momentary sense of satisfaction that she had displeased the perfect Judith, but a feeling of guilt quickly replaced it. Once again, she was letting her friends down.

This bouncing back and forth between emotions was not something that Marsha liked about herself. Of course, the list of what she didn't like about herself, or anyone else, was much longer than what she did.

There were only a few things that Marsha felt she did well. One was worrying. About everything. Today she was worrying about school. She liked it, and she hated it. Shouldn't she like all parts of it?

Bree said no, nobody had to enjoy all the things about school. After their first two years of college were over and they had taken the classes they had to take, Marsha would be free to take more of what she wanted.

Besides, since their pact to stay in town only lasted through the first two years of school, she could also go anywhere she wanted to go after that.

"But I don't know what I want," Marsha would say so quietly that Bree would have to bend in to hear.

"I'm sure you do," Bree would answer. "You just haven't let yourself want it yet."

Marsha would turn away, knowing that Bree was probably right as she usually was, but that didn't help. She still didn't know. It made her laugh inside to know that most people read her independence as confidence when mostly it was confusion.

Stuffing the book into her already overflowing backpack, Marsha hurried out of the library to meet her friends. As she passed the large glass door, she caught a reflection of herself. Tall, thin, a dancer's body. Nothing she had to work for. But she worked hard at being a dancer, and that was where she found herself at peace.

Maybe Bree was right. She did know what she wanted, and she was only afraid because she wouldn't find it in this podunk town. Losing her friends seemed like too high a price to pay to do what she wanted to do in life.

The library and the campus HUB were nearby, but even though she felt guilty for being late, Marsha didn't hurry. She dawdled, as her mother would have said. It was a habit she had developed young, not knowing what would greet her when she got home.

Sometimes her mother was in the kitchen making her a snack. Other days, Marsha would open the door and find her mother passed out on the floor. Marsha's heart would race. She'd rush to her mother to see if she was still breathing, and since she always was, the wave of adrenaline that fueled her fear would sweep into anger or depression.

Other times Marsha would open the door to a screaming lunatic and quickly back out before her crazy mother trapped her. Before she found Bree and her circle of friends, she would hide in the backyard, swatting at bugs in the summer and trying to stay warm in the winter, waiting for the manic version of her mother to be over.

So she walked slowly, fully aware that her friends weren't her mother, but also knowing that she had probably disappointed them again. Still, they never held it against her. Even Judith never let her anger linger. She reminded herself that they were her safe space and hurried through the hall to the coffee shop, almost bumping into Mr. Hunky professor, who looked as panicked as she felt.

Wonder what that's about, Marsha thought, as she looked for her friends.

She saw them across the room. Their heads bent forward, giggling together. Cindy looked up and saw her and waved her over while practically hopping out of her chair in anticipation.

"What's going on?" Marsha asked.

"Bree met the man she is going to marry!" April giggled.

"She says she is going to marry him," Judith corrected.

"She will. You know she knows these things." Cindy answered.

Marsha looked at Bree, leaning back in her chair, smiling. "Is it true?"

"It is!" Bree said, grabbing Marsha's hand and pulling her down to the empty seat beside her.

"Who are you going to marry?"

This time Cindy couldn't help herself. She almost tipped over her chair in her excitement. "Professor Hunky!"

Six

Current time...

"Professor Hunky," Bree said out loud to herself, remembering that day.

She had been radiant, knowing that her future lay before her, bright and shining. Her friends laughing, believing her because she had so often known things before them and was so often right, but mostly because it sounded like a fairy tale.

They had all believed in them back then, devouring Disney movies and happy endings like candy. They would whisper to each other about their dreams of a fairy tale life during their many sleepovers.

But that was then. This was now. And now Bree knew there were no such things as fairy tales. She knew they had all missed the fact that the stories never told you what happened after the prince and princess got married. Now she knew what happened. They get old and one of them dies. After all, that's what happened to her.

What really made her mad was the fact that she hadn't died. It should have been her. It would have been easier for Paul. He had friends, work, and travel, and women would be again crawling out of the woodwork if Hunky Professor was free again.

Instead, he had died, and she had nothing. Instead, here she was still sitting with her back up against the door, holding the letter with stickers all over it to make sure she noticed and didn't throw it into the junk pile.

Did he expect her to keep going on as usual? Did Paul expect she would continue to get the mail every day, go through it, sorting, filing, and taking care of things? Perhaps he did. On the other hand, he made sure his letter stood out, just in case she wasn't wholly herself after he died.

Idiot, she thought. *Of course, I wouldn't be.*

Yes, she had married Professor Hunky, who had let her down and died. And now she had nothing and nobody. It was the same story she had been telling herself every day for the past month. While he was sick, she didn't have time to think. She had him to take care of, and then he took that away too.

But that letter was making her curious. And she knew Paul would have counted on that. Her curiosity and her need to solve puzzles in life. So now, despite herself, she could feel a desire to do something returning. She tried to will it away. This dreamy, depressed, lonely state had become a safe place to live, and she didn't want it to slip away all because of the letter.

Sighing, Bree leaned back against the door, still on the floor surrounded by mail and a letter that wouldn't leave her alone. She would have to open it at some point. Just not now. She wasn't ready.

Besides, she had to go to the bathroom, a much more current problem than the one she was stuck in. Plus, she was hungry. That she was hungry was also new. She had forced herself to eat something every day, knowing that despite her complete lack of desire to do anything or see anybody, she wouldn't be dying anytime soon.

But hungry had not been part of the equation before. However, hungry or not, she knew she didn't have the energy to eat anything other than the food bars and frozen vegetables she had been eating for the last month. And she was sick of them. She finally wanted something different.

As Bree shuffled to the bathroom, she knocked over a pile of mail, and it irritated her. There it was again, a feeling she hadn't had since Paul had died. Dismay over disorder. And also the pain.

The pain that she had deadened, hiding from it, was sticking its head up, reminding her that although Paul had gone away, the pain was still there. What was different was now she was ready to admit that perhaps it was possible to feel the pain and live again.

Leaning against the sink in the bathroom she had so carefully designed, she stared into the mirror at herself and started to cry again. Perhaps she had died but had gone to hell. Her hair, usually short, sassy, and silky, now looked like straw pieces.

And her skin, to which she had so carefully applied creams and lotions, was gray and covered with little red bumps, probably from not washing it for days. Dark blue circles lay under her eyes, and her eyes were now so bloodshot they looked red. All that work, keeping herself beautiful for Paul, had disappeared along with him.

However, the unfamiliar feeling of hunger was growing stronger. Bree knew she couldn't go out looking like this, but she could order pizza. Opening her office door—where she had once spent most of her days but hadn't seen since she had taken care of everything she needed to do after Paul died—she found her phone charging by her computer. Thanking her past self for at least taking care of that bit, she pulled up their favorite pizza shop and ordered—a whole pizza just for her, something new. Also new, no meat on half of it.

Just that realization was almost enough to send her back to the floor, but the letter was waiting. And she needed to be ready to read it, which meant a shower and food.

Thirty minutes later, feeling marginally better, Bree handed the pizza delivery woman enough money to cover the pizza and a generous tip and was grateful that it wasn't the usual boy who delivered when Paul was alive.

Bree almost asked where he was, her curiosity driving her again, but instead ducked her head and mumbled thank you. But not so soon that she didn't notice the dismay in the young girl's eyes as she glimpsed the mess lying on the floor behind her and Bree's gray face.

Before she could say anything, Bree stopped her by saying, "I'm fine, just getting over something."

The girl nodded, said thank you, and turned away. But Bree, watching through the peephole, saw her turn back to the door as if she wanted to knock again and make sure, but shook her head and headed back to her car.

Of course, the girl knew what had happened. She and Paul were regulars at the pizza shop. Someone would have told them why they had stopped coming in. She should have thought to order from someplace else.

Paul had remained the hunky professor, and even though he wasn't the best conversationalist, often in his head figuring out something or other, he was always kind and ready to help others. He had told her they remembered them because of her. She was outgoing and curious. She didn't believe him.

But there it was again, the feeling of curiosity, waking her up and moving her forward into life. To defeat it, at least for now, she put the letter on her desk, made sure the phone volume was still turned off so she would not hear or see the messages that she knew had piled up, and closed the door again.

All of it could wait until after she ate and maybe watched a movie, just like they used to do. For the past month, she had felt nothing. Now she felt hunger, pain, and dread that the letter would tell her something she didn't want to know. She would put it off for a few more hours.

Seven

B ree woke to the sun streaming through the crack in the curtain she had left while looking at the mailman. She moaned, rolled, and almost fell off the couch. The TV was playing in the background. A pizza box lay open on the coffee table, one slice left with wilted vegetables and cheese strings hanging off the edges.

She didn't know what part of the morning was most disturbing—the fact that the sun was up, that she had fallen asleep on the couch, that the TV was on, or that last piece of pizza. Nothing had ever happened in her life when any of those events had transpired, especially all at once. But Bree decided that the last piece of pizza was the worst part. How had she eaten a whole pizza by herself and yet was still hungry?

A few minutes later, she was in front of her bathroom mirror, staring at her image again. At least her skin wasn't as gray, and her hazel eyes looked a little brighter and a little less red.

Perhaps one night like that isn't such a terrible thing, Bree thought.

At least she felt like doing something, and that feeling had been missing for so long she had thought it had died along with Paul.

After a shower, fresh clothes, and a cup of coffee in her hand, Bree stared at her bedroom. She hadn't slept in that bed since Paul had started sleeping on a hospital bed they installed in his office, pushing his desk with all the papers to the side of the room.

She had brought the cot in that they had used years before when they went on a road trip and slept there, sometimes holding his hand, hoping it would help them both sleep.

For a few days after his death, she was her usual orderly self. Holding herself together, she had the hospital bed removed and took care of Paul's cremation. One of Paul's colleagues put together a gathering, and she shook the hands of some people and hugged others, barely registering what she was saying or who was standing in front of her.

Afterward, she took the box home with her and stuffed it under the bed, unwilling to think about the fact that the man who had filled up her entire life was now nothing more than ashes. And then she returned to the cot in Paul's office and gave up.

Now, as she stared at the bed, everything perfect, just as she had left it before moving onto the cot, Bree wondered if she could ever sleep in it again. If by chance his scent had remained after she washed the sheets before making the bed that last time—what was she thinking when she did that—would it comfort her? She didn't think so.

Actually, she wasn't even sure if she could stay in the house. Or the town. The urge to run away from life had kept her housebound and closed up these last thirty days. Now she wanted to run from this life.

But where would she go? What would she do? When Paul had gotten sick, she told her agent she was done writing. The company that managed marketing her book sales functioned well without her, and even if all of it died away, she didn't care. Without Paul, she knew her desire to write was over.

What life did she want to live now? She did not know. And she still had a letter to open.

Sighing, she crossed the hall to her office and stepped in, this time allowing herself to notice the mess. She hated mess. But the closed door had kept it out of her sight and her thoughts. Now, more cleared-sighted than she had been for months, she saw what she had left undone the day she had canceled everyone and closed her computer.

There was dust everywhere, which became more visible when she raised the blinds and let in the sun. The clutter and dirt screamed at her, as it always did, to do something. but the loudest noise was coming from the letter, still lying on top of the papers where she had left it after ordering pizza.

It was yelling, "Open, open, open."

It reminded her of the Mervyn's Department Stores commercial in the early '90s, where the woman stood pressed against the store window saying, "Open, open, open," waiting to get into their super sale. Except then, it was about finding something exciting. And the letter couldn't possibly hold anything exciting.

Perhaps the letter contained a confession of some kind. If so, Bree didn't want to hear it. Paul wasn't perfect, but the one thing she had held to was he had always, always, been loyal and faithful to her. If it turned out that he hadn't been, she was sure it would kill her, and despite how she had been living the last thirty days, she knew she didn't want to die yet.

Not that she knew what she wanted to do. She didn't need money. She had enough of her own, and she knew Paul had life insurance. A lot of it. He had promised her he would take care of her forever, and that was one of the first things he had done right after they had married.

Bree gasped at the idea. Had he known he had some disease and would leave her this way? Way back then? No, it wasn't possible. He could never have gotten the insurance. Besides, who would know that they would get cancer? No one. Right?

Right, she said to herself. Eventually, she had to open the letter, check her phone, and read her email—all daunting tasks. But after doing those things, maybe she would know what to do with her life.

But first, she had to clean up the office. And the idea that she would clean it up as if she was packing everything away gave her the impetus that she needed. And since it wasn't as bad as she first thought, given that she had always kept things orderly before Paul got sick, she finished the basics within a few hours.

Everything was sorted—piles of papers she needed to shred and items she needed to throw away. Plus a pile of stuff that she wasn't sure what to do about yet. The phone and the computer she left for later. She still wasn't ready to face that much of the world.

But now that the office was back to its normal orderly state, the letter sat by itself in the center of the curved desk that always gave her plenty of room to spread out as she worked, and then drawers to file everything away when she finished.

It looked ridiculous sitting there. She felt stupid for being afraid of a letter covered with stickers. But she was. And she knew she needed to do one more thing before she read it. Eat. Again.

She had stopped her hunger for a few hours drinking coffee, but now she needed food. Once again, she picked up her phone and ordered. This time her favorite Thai food. Feeling no guilt for not cooking, she walked to the kitchen, pulled everything out of her refrigerator that probably wasn't good anymore, and threw it into the trash.

After tipping the Door Dash driver, she took the containers of curry and rice, grabbed a soda, and stepped outside onto the deck that overlooked their small backyard.

Thirty minutes later, after some fresh air, a little sun, and good food, she was ready to tackle the letter.

What Bree didn't know was her letter was not the only letter Paul had sent. She would find out later what he had been up to months before he had let her know how sick he was.

How many trips he had taken without her, and how many plans he had made.

If she had known that day, she might have never opened the letter because it would reveal that Paul had kept secrets from her.

Bree might not have understood that he had done it for what he considered the best reason of all. Because she was the love of his life, and he knew he was leaving her.

That day in the hall, after watching her watch him, seeing her friends turn and stare, Paul knew the life he had planned, the life he had known, was over, and he had begun planning a new one. Of course, even though he was full of trepidation, it had never occurred to him it would not last forever.

Eight

S he had brought the mail in last night but hadn't had time to sort it. Now, standing at the kitchen counter, Cindy stared at the letter in her hand, the return address showing a name she hadn't seen for so many years: Paul Stanford Mann.

Well, that wasn't entirely true. She had seen his name on the Internet. They even friended each other, and she wished him and Bree happy birthday every time their birthdays came around. Even though they never responded, she did it anyway.

Just thinking about Bree made Cindy want to cry. Best friends for years, and then, nothing. The girl who had hidden in the cloakroom and then reached out to another frightened child had disappeared. And after all these years, Cindy still didn't know why.

One day, Paul and Bree were a huge part of all their lives, and then they weren't. It was as if she, their friends, and the town, never existed for Bree and Paul. They moved, never came back, contacted no one, and became invisible.

Years later, social media came along, and one day, still missing her best friend, Cindy searched for them. She found Paul and learned where the two of them had gone. Paul was no longer teaching. He was working for a company.

Cindy figured that was probably the only reason he was on social media since there was hardly anything personal about him in his profile. Bree was nowhere to be found, only the mention that he was married, and Cindy assumed that meant he remained married to Bree.

Still, she had hoped that when she found Paul, he would tell Bree, and they could all be friends again. Maybe not as before, but at least they could reunite online. And although Paul had friended her back, that was the end of their contact.

Cindy suspected Paul had friended her automatically, not realizing who she was. Friends on Facebook differed from real friends. On social media, friends were people who might know your name. Nothing more.

So now, after all her unacknowledged birthday greetings, there was a letter?

It was so improbable that all Cindy could do was stare at it. Just holding it sent a chill down her spine, and a flurry of questions ran through her thoughts. Why a letter? What happened?

But before she could either open the letter or run a search on the Internet, her phone pinged in the other room. Now she knew where she had left it. She always put it down somewhere and had to wait for it to ring to find it, sometimes resorting to asking "Alexa" to call her phone.

A glance at the kitchen clock told her she would be late meeting Judith, and Judith still hated people not being on time. She and Judith had a standing Monday morning coffee before both of them started their workweek. They were the only two of the pact of friends who had stayed in town. The group had slowly dissipated. Bree and Paul were the last to go.

Marsha left as soon as she could, surprising no one. Everyone knew she wanted much more than could be found in tiny Spring Falls, a Pennsylvania town in what Marsha said was in the middle of nowhere.

Marsha had spent a few years trying to make it on Broadway. She had been in a few plays, singing and dancing in the chorus, but eventually realized she would never be good enough and left New York.

Through Judith, Cindy knew that Marsha now ran a small dance school and had never married. Or if she had, no one knew about it.

April had eloped with a boy she met in history class after graduating from the community college and then they moved away. April kept in touch with Judith, and through her, Cindy knew April had two children and was expecting a grandchild from the oldest.

As Cindy drove to the coffee shop to meet Judith, the unopened letter in her purse, Cindy thought about all that the five of them had gone through together, and all the promises they had made to each other, but never really kept.

For years she had known Bree as well as she knew herself. She knew Bree's secrets, even the ones she never shared.

That was one thing about Bree everyone accepted. She was private and rarely shared, even with her best friends. The other thing about Bree was once she decided, she did what she said she would do. She said she and Paul would marry, and they did.

They had waited until Bree graduated from the community college before officially dating since Paul wanted to keep his job, and couldn't date a student. But no one missed the looks they gave each other in the meantime.

Then they waited a more few months before Bree moved into Paul's small apartment. Bree didn't want to go on to university because it would mean leaving Paul. Paul kept teaching, and Bree took multiple odd jobs trying to find something that fit her.

Cindy lost count of how many jobs Bree had during that year. After a while, Cindy knew that word got around that Bree was a hard worker, but wouldn't stay if the reins were held too tightly, and it got harder and harder for Bree to find work.

Bree said she didn't care. She told her friends she was preparing for a future and just needed experiences. Besides, she was planning a wedding.

A year after Bree graduated, she and Paul married. Cindy, Judith, April, and Marsha had all been her bridesmaids. Actually, they had made up almost the entire wedding party.

April's husband, Ron Page, had been Paul's best man, mainly because Paul couldn't think of who else to ask. Besides being April's husband, Ron had been a student of Paul's. And since Paul said he had no family to invite, Ron was the easiest choice.

Paul explained that he never met the few cousins he had. Besides, they were scattered across the country. And he had been an only child. Both parents had died while he was away at college.

Bree's mother had given her away and then beamed at her only child, tears running down her face as she sat with some of the parents of Bree's best friends.

As small as it had been, the wedding was perfect and lovely. Of course, Bree had planned it down to the smallest detail, and they had all happily gone along with everything, delighted to be together.

Marsha had flown in from New York, looking very sophisticated, and April and Ron had driven in from where they were living. April was already pregnant with her first child, which made finding a bridesmaid dress difficult. Bree finally picked a color and let everyone choose the dress they wanted to wear. Bree paid for the dresses out of the money she had earned working all her odd jobs.

They put Ron in charge of making sure Paul had a boy's night out, which consisted of drinking beer at the local pub and watching football. Thinking about that made Cindy chuckle. None of them had been party people even then. Now they were considered middle-aged and definitely not party people. What they were, she wasn't sure.

A single tear ran down her cheek, and she brushed it away, angry at herself again for missing what never happened. She had thought the five of them would be friends for life. People she could count on, precious friends who would always reach their hands out to her. And none of that had happened.

As Cindy parked, she saw Judith through the glass window of the coffee shop waiting for her, early as usual. Which meant it wasn't true that none of that had happened. There was always Judith. Her fearless friend. And that friend was holding a letter in her hand and waving it at her.

Almost falling out of her car in her excitement, Cindy pulled her letter out of her purse and waved it back. Judith stood as Cindy came through the door, and they stared at each other.

"I texted you. You didn't answer!" Judith said.

"Rushing to get here!"

Both of them, holding up the letters, asked at the same time, "What do these mean?"

Nine

"We all got one?" Cindy said in surprise. "All of us?"
"That's what he said," Judith answered.

They had opened their letters at the same time, and now the single sheets of paper lay on the table in front of them, giving them no answers, only questions.

Just then, Judith's phone pinged.

"It's from April. She wants to know what we are supposed to do."

Cindy's mind drifted back to the coat closet and how Bree had reached out to her and how their friendship had made school a safe space for her. For all of them, really. Bree had held them together.

Perhaps it was time for them to do precisely what Paul had asked them to do—begged, really.

"Do what he asked," Cindy finally said, and once she said it, she knew it was the right thing.

"But the gallery?" Judith said. "What will you do with it?"

"It will take me a few days to get things in order. My assistants, Janet and Mimi, can run it while I'm gone. Will you check in and make sure they are doing okay? Get them more help if they need it?"

Cindy knew that would be a piece of cake in Judith's world. Judith, who had grown into a strong, independent, and self-assured woman, was one of the town leaders. She ran an accounting firm, and her staff did the bookkeeping and taxes for more than half the businesses in town, including Cindy's art gallery.

Although she had never married, Judith always had a date when she wanted one, which was rare. She told Cindy that all the men she dated eventually wanted her to be a "little woman," and that was something she would never be.

Sometimes they didn't even know that's what they wanted, but it always came out in little ways, and she would never allow herself to give in to that stereotype of a woman.

Judith's flaming red hair had softened, but not her determination. Cindy loved how kind and generous Judith was, but she also knew that it was wise never to cross her or do something blatantly wrong on purpose.

The town council had more than once done battle with Judith, and they always lost in the end. Cindy wondered why they just didn't do what Judith suggested in the first place.

When Judith brought a suggestion to the council, it had already been researched and studied. Yes, a light was needed on that road. No, it was wrong to use a trash company that didn't actually recycle, no matter how much money they had donated to the town's maintenance fund.

"Of course, I will," Judith said. "What else do you want me to do?"

"Well, I suppose we better find Marsha and make sure she opened her letter and will do what he asks of us."

Judith laughed, "That's just like Marsha, always the one we have to track down."

"True," Cindy laughed. "On the other hand, she always comes through."

• • • ● •● • ● • •• •

At that moment, Marsha was sitting cross-legged on the floor of her dance studio with the letter lying open on her lap. She leaned back against the mirror, enjoying how cool it felt on her back.

The air smelled of dust. The rosin from the box in the corner was scattered across the floor because she hadn't bothered to sweep it up after the last ballet class. She had let things fall apart at the studio. She wasn't even sure why. All she knew was nothing felt right anymore. It wasn't just one of her moods. It was something else.

Marsha thought back to the day she had first met Bree. A new dance teacher had come to town, and Marsha had begged her mother to let her take lessons.

In one of her few lucid moments, her mother said it was alright with her, but they didn't have enough money to pay for it.

Marsha remembered thinking that if her mother didn't drink as much as she did, there would be plenty of money. But she kept her mouth shut and told her mother she'd figure out a way to pay for it herself.

Her mother had sighed, said that she had always wanted to be a dancer, took a long look at the daughter standing in front of her as if seeing her for the first time, and said, "I'll pay for the first month. See if you like it. After that, you pay for it."

Marsha hadn't hesitated. She'd figure out a way to pay for the lessons. All she wanted was a chance to start.

BECA LEWIS

But looking back, she wondered what was her mother thinking? She was only ten years old. How could she pay for her lessons? The answer was—her mother wasn't thinking. She never did.

But she kept her promise about paying for the first month of lessons, and Marsha had walked into that studio and immediately felt safe and secure.

It took only one class before Marsha knew she had found something she could count on to make her happy. But that day, she found something else she could count on—a friend. After class, Bree came up to her, told her she was a really good dancer, and asked if Marsha had taken lessons before.

"No," Marsha had answered.

"Well, this seems like your thing then, doesn't it?" Bree had replied.

That was Bree. She knew right away what your gift was, and she would encourage and support it if you let her.

She helped Marsha figure out ways to pay for classes. Sometimes they both washed the studio windows, mirrors, and floors in exchange for classes for Marsha. Bree never asked for herself.

Even though Bree's mother was a space case, and often Bree was on her own, Bree always figured out a way to make things work.

Now it was Bree who needed help. *Of course, she hadn't asked for it,* Marsha thought. If Paul hadn't told them, they would have never known.

Marsha looked around her studio and let herself cry. She was lonely. She missed her friends. She missed Bree especially. All these years had gone by, and she hadn't really tried to find out what had happened to her. They had all let her drift away.

When her phone rang, Marsha said "yes," even before Cindy asked the question.

After hanging up, Marsha stood, stretched, took another look around the studio, and made up her mind. She would accept the offer and sell. It was time to go home.

Neither Bree, April, Judith, Cindy, nor Marsha knew Paul had sent one more letter.

Grace Strong saw it drop through her mail slot and noticed it right away. Even without the stickers, she would have noticed. Grace often said she didn't have any magical gifts, and that she was no one special, but she possessed a strong intuitive sense about things, and as the bills and junk mail fell to the floor, she knew there was something in that pile that needed her immediate attention.

Putting down her coffee cup and her morning scone, Grace waved to the mail carrier through the window of her coffee shop, opened the door to the pass-through space that kept the elements out, picked up the mail, and took it back to her table.

The early morning crowd had come and gone, but a few people were chatting in the corner, and others were working on computers. It was just as she had always envisioned her coffee shop-book-store would look. Grace sighed with happiness. She had made a life for herself in a town that she loved.

Grace sorted through the mail, took out the junk pieces to be put in the recycle bin, and moved the bills to one side for her bookkeeper, which left the letter sitting by itself in the middle of the table.

The name Paul Stanford Mann was on the return label. It had been forty-six years since she had seen that name and never expected to see it again.

With trembling hands, she opened the letter and then understood why she had a hunch about it. Yes, this was another adventure. But not the kind that would involve her new home or her current friends. This adventure was about the past and was not coming to her. She would be going to it.

Ten

B ree stared at the unopened letter and wondered where it
would be best to open it. Here in her now tidy office? Or the
living room where they watched TV and ate lunch together when
Paul was home?

When he wasn't home, she'd read a book while she ate, always
eating more than she wanted to because she didn't want to stop
reading.

Or perhaps she'd open it outside in the garden on the bench
under the tree. Bree decided against the garden because she hadn't
been outside since Paul died, and she knew all she would see was
work that needed to be done to bring the garden back to health.

No, she thought. It made sense to open the letter where she
wrote and ran her business. That way, perhaps she could read the
letter without becoming too emotional.

"Yea, right," she said out loud.

Reaching into her desk drawer, she took out her letter opener
and, after pausing once more, slit the top of the envelope and
pulled out the letter.

Although stickers of flowers, birds, trees, and hearts plastered the envelope, the letter was a sheet of plain white paper. Bree recognized Paul's precise printing and, of course, his sprawling signature after the last line, which she read first as she always did.

You were and always will be the love and light of my life. Yours, forever, Paul

"Yea, right," Bree said again out loud. "That's why you left me all alone."

Bree knew she was being unreasonable. It wasn't his fault that he died. But after reading the entire letter, she felt even angrier.

Her first impulse was to tear it into tiny bits or take it directly to the shredder. But she didn't.

Instead, she left the letter lying in the middle of the desk, stood, grabbed her keys, and left the house for the first time in a month. She had planned to take the car and start driving—somewhere, anywhere—but when she opened the garage door and a blast of air carrying the scent of spring flowers rushed in, she decided to walk instead.

But first, she grabbed her hat and sunglasses, disguising herself as much as possible, hoping none of her neighbors would recognize her so she could remain inside her shell.

The truth is, Bree thought as she turned the corner heading for the park a few blocks away, *they probably wouldn't recognize me anyway, and for sure they don't know me.*

That had been her intention, hadn't it? To be invisible? No one but Paul and the people she worked with knew that she was R.B. Curtis, a well-known romance writer. R for her first name, Rhoberta. But she never used that name, going by her middle name, Bree, instead. The C was for Curtis, her maiden name. Yes, her circle of friends knew her last name of Curtis, but there were lots of people named Curtis.

Bree knew her mother had named her Rhoberta after her own mother, trying to make her mother happy because she had gotten pregnant by one of the many boys she had "goofed around with." Bree never knew who her father was, even though she had begged to know. Probably her mother didn't even know.

Yes, she had also tried to please her mother, which was a lost cause. Her mother remained locked in her past and drank herself to death shortly after the wedding.

Thankfully, her mother was fairly sober on Bree's wedding day, and her mother walking her down the aisle was one of Bree's treasured memories. She was also grateful that her mother had not seen what happened after she married or who she had become herself.

Not a drunk like her mother. Instead, she had become a recluse, hiding from the world and the pain it contained, making up her own world where everything was perfect.

She and Marsha had recognized that in each other. Although they each handled an out-of-control mother and absent and non-existent father differently, it was another thing that had bound them together.

A sob caught Bree by surprise. Stumbling to a park bench hidden partly by a newly blooming lilac bush, she realized she had opened a door she had shut years before. And now there they were, back in her mind. Her friends. The safe space.

Paul had done it. She knew that's what he intended. And although she wanted to hate him or scream at him for doing it, she knew he meant it to be a last gift to her.

It was a gift that she had a choice to accept or not. But if she did, it was going to open up old wounds.

"Although it might open up old joys, too," Bree heard.

It was as if the wind moving through the lilacs had brought the words Paul might have spoken along with the lilac's unique and unforgettable scent.

It's hard to feel angry around a lilac, Bree thought.

And then she let herself look around. The entire park was awash in the colors of spring. Winter was over. The question Bree had to answer for herself was if she was willing for her winter to be over, too. And if she was, what would she become?

Would her friends forgive her? Would she ever forgive herself?

A hummingbird, maybe fresh from his long trip, hovered directly in front of Bree's face, her body hovering between furiously beating wings. The two stared at each other, and then the hummingbird dipped, turned, and flew to the bush, wings still beating the air, the soft sound they made filling Bree's heart.

She knew the hummingbird was a harbinger of things to come. Bree leaned back against the bench, lifted her face to the sky, and let the sun beat down on her face. Eyes closed, she saw the letter again in her mind's eye.

She saw Paul's words, "Yours forever," and decided to believe them. At least for now.

Eleven

Cindy paced back and forth as she waited for her flight. It had taken her more than a few days to arrange the trip. She had been so excited when she first got the idea, but now she was worrying. What if Bree didn't want to see her? What if she had already left?

It doesn't matter, Cindy told herself. She, along with Judith, Marsha, and April, were determined, and no matter what, they would find Bree and do what Paul asked them to do.

However, as determined as Cindy felt, she was still full of anxiety, trying to plan out all the ways that things could go wrong and what she would do to fix them.

The airport was hot, crowded, and full of smells she didn't like, which didn't help. So she followed her nose to the one wonderful smell, the Cinnabon store, hoping that a bun and coffee would make things better. They did for a moment. Then the worry started again.

Had Bree read the letter? Would she like what it said? Would Bree wait? Would Bree know it was Cindy who would come? Was she the wrong person to help? Maybe someone stronger like Judith or more independent like Marsha would be better.

Cindy's thoughts whirled around like a tornado, gathering up bits and pieces of all her fears and flinging them at her. What would Bree do when she showed up at her house? Would she slam the door in her face? Isn't that what she had done for all these years? Shut them all out. Why would she let them in again?

Cindy recognized that the string of worrying what-if thoughts were not helping. They made everything worse, and she willed herself to stop. She pulled out a book, hoping it would sweep her away into a different world, but she couldn't focus on the words.

Worrying is sometimes valuable, Cindy told herself.

But she knew that was only when she let the worry carry her to solutions. It was how she opened her art gallery and made it successful despite it being a small town with apparently very little interest in art. But once there was a place to see art, the artists in town came forward, and now there was a thriving arts community in Spring Falls.

Thinking about the gallery helped calm her nerves. She was so proud of it. The gallery provided an outlet for artists not only in town but also worldwide. The Internet had been the solution. Remembering that, Cindy knew that just as there had been a solution then, there would be a solution now to whatever happened with Bree.

Besides, Paul had insisted that they could reach into Bree's pain and pull her back into the world. He didn't tell them why he and Bree had left town. Nor explain why Bree had stopped talking to them once they disappeared.

All he had said was Bree's secrets were not for him to tell. But if they did what he asked of them, he was sure that Bree would find happiness again. And that was all that was important to him.

After they realized that all four had received letters from Paul, Judith had arranged a Zoom call for them. Seeing her friend's faces all in one place almost brought Cindy to tears. And when Marsha told them she was moving back home, Cindy did burst into tears, which took Marsha entirely by surprise.

"I'm so happy," Cindy said.

"You are happy I am coming home?" Marsha asked.

It wasn't until that moment that Marsha realized how worried she had been about her announcement. She had been distant from them for so long she didn't know if they cared anymore. Actually, she knew she had always worried that they didn't care. It's what she told herself to keep from feeling homesick.

"Yes," Cindy sobbed, Judith nodded yes with tears in her eyes, and Marsha surprised herself by crying too.

"I am thinking these are all happy tears?" April had asked, tears in her own eyes, thinking how much she missed her friends and wondering what it would be like to go home too. But she couldn't. Ron would never approve.

They spent their time on that first call alternating between laughing and crying and doing their best to avoid anything unpleasant. But all of them agreed that their priority was to help Bree.

Before Cindy left town, they had another Zoom call to plan what to do after Cindy contacted Bree, although they couldn't plan much. All they knew was that there would be no more letters. Instead, Paul said he had left clues for Bree. Paul knew she loved to figure things out. He wanted her to live again. And she loved surprises. At least she had used to love them.

So he had carefully planned his last gift to her. It was like a scavenger hunt. And he promised them all that if they followed the clues, Bree would find happiness again.

"I beg you," he had written to each of them."Don't give up. Please help me give this gift to Bree. And to all of you."

The first step on this scavenger hunt was Bree. Go to her. She had the first clue in her letter.

And the most obvious person to go was Cindy. After all, it was Bree and Cindy who had been friends first. It was Bree who had reached her hand out to Cindy as she huddled in the coat closet.

Now Cindy would reach out to Bree, who had been hiding from them for far too long.

Twelve

C indy paid the Uber driver, having asked him to drop her off a few blocks from Bree's house.

"I want to surprise my friend," Cindy told him. "It's been almost thirty years since we've seen each other."

"Why did you wait so long?" he asked, looking at Cindy in the rearview mirror.

"I didn't know where she lived."

The driver paused long enough for Cindy to hear what she had said. *How could she have let that be an excuse*, she asked herself.

As if he heard her thoughts, the driver said, "At least you are here now. It must be when she needs you the most. There's a park a few blocks from that address. Do you want me to drop you there? Perhaps some time under the trees will supply you with the courage you are seeking?"

His kindness and understanding rendered Cindy incapable of speaking, so she nodded yes. She resisted hugging him as he held the door for her, not knowing if he would like it.

Instead, she smiled, said thank you, and turned to look at the park that was filled with light filtering through the new leaves on the trees. A light breeze brought a hint of lilacs and daffodils. She breathed deeply, and some of her worries vanished.

She had packed lightly, as Paul had suggested. They could buy what they needed as they traveled. His attorney, Bruce Dawson, would make sure they had all the funds they needed to do what he requested.

Judith had contacted the attorney and had him wire funds to an account that all four of them could access as needed during the scavenger hunt. The attorney had refused to give them any information, only telling them that Paul had asked him to provide them with whatever they needed, and yes, he had been the one to mail the letters. Just before hanging up, he had wished them good luck.

"Good luck!" the Uber driver said as he set her small piece of luggage on the sidewalk. He, like the attorney, didn't add, "You'll need it," but that's what Cindy heard behind the words. Yes, she would need it.

Cindy let her gaze travel around the park, looking for a place to sit and think. Halfway around the park, she stopped, her breath catching in her throat and her heart beating so fast she thought she might faint.

It seemed impossible. It probably was. But sitting on a bench only a few feet away was a woman whose profile, although much older, was the same profile she had seen every day as she sat beside it in elementary school.

One breath later, the woman turned, saw Cindy, stood, stared, and within seconds both women ran towards each other, the suitcase dropping to the ground unnoticed.

Clutching each other, they sobbed, and then laughed, sobbed again, and finally, it was Bree who said, "I had hoped it was you who would come."

Hours later, the two of them were in Bree's living room. Another box of pizza had been delivered and eaten. Bree had set Cindy up in the guest bedroom, and now that they were both full, it was time to talk.

Cindy knew it was probably the wrong place to start, but her heart had broken when Bree left, so she had to ask.

"Why did you leave, Bree?"

"I can't tell you that."

"Why?"

Bree sighed and looked away. The moment she saw Cindy standing on the sidewalk, it was as if all the years apart had fallen away, and they were young again and ready for the world. But the wall she had around her had only gotten stronger through the years, and she knew she couldn't take it down. At least not now. Maybe never.

"Can we not talk about that?"

Cindy nodded. She had loved Bree despite that wall before. Now that they were together again, Cindy wasn't about to let Bree's wall get in the way of their friendship.

The one thing she knew about Bree was that she always tried to do the right thing. So whatever had happened, it wasn't something Bree did wrong, although she probably felt that she had.

"Okay," Cindy said, putting her empty soda can down and tucking her feet up. "Let's talk about when we are going to leave."

Bree glanced at her hands, wondering how long the brown spots had been there, took a deep breath, and said, "Don't know if I am going to."

"It's what Paul wanted."

"What about what I want?" Bree said, almost shouting.

59

"What's going on, Bree. You always do what you want. That's your thing. You told me that. So why do I hear anger about what Paul wanted?"

Bree stood. "Just tired, I suppose. Can we talk about this later?"

"No," Cindy answered, surprising even herself. "We can't. I get that you don't want to talk about what happened before, but now I won't have it. I'm here because Paul asked us to be with you on this crazy scavenger hunt. Despite you not being around for the last thirty years, we are all willing to stop what we are doing and be here for you.

"So no, we can't talk about this later. And really, now that I think about it, you don't have a choice. This trip is something you will do whether or not you like it. Sit down. Let's plan."

Bree stared at her friend, turned away, and then started laughing.

"What!" Cindy demanded, now furious with herself for having a hissy fit and Bree for laughing.

Bree shook her head, still laughing, and said, "You have become someone, Cindy, and I am so proud of you."

Cindy stared at Bree, realized what she said was true, and that set off another round of hugging and laughing.

After a few minutes, Cindy said, "Well, thanks, I think. But I'm serious. When are we leaving? And he said you have the first clue. What is it?"

Thirteen

The next morning, Bree woke up in a bad mood. She couldn't answer Cindy's question. She did not know what the clue was that Paul said she had. And she had dreamed that she lived in a pink cloud. That vision of life was so far removed from the life she had now, it made her feel angry and frustrated.

Bree hated being angry and frustrated, even though those feelings overrode some of the grief that greeted her with every breath. However, Bree knew that being angry and frustrated meant she would be snappy and rude to Cindy, who certainly didn't deserve it.

But then, Bree thought, *she's known me a long time. Perhaps she'll forgive me.*

Bree put aside the nagging voice that reminded her she had often asked Cindy and the girls to forgive her for a lot more than her snappy, snarky nature and headed to the kitchen to make coffee, hoping Cindy wasn't up yet. She enjoyed being by herself.

Even when Paul was alive, she enjoyed the time he went off on trips or worked all day. The difference was he would come home, and they talked and shared what they did while he was gone. Now he would never return home again.

She wasn't so lucky. Cindy was already in the kitchen making coffee. She had just shut the refrigerator door when Bree walked in, and she gave Bree a long cool look.

"What have you been eating? Or not eating? There's nothing in there or in the cupboards."

"Bars and frozen vegetables. All gone now, though."

"Perhaps we need to go grocery shopping?"

Bree took the coffee Cindy had made, sipped, and said, "You remembered how I like my coffee."

"I remember many things, Bree. And one of them is that you don't like to talk about yourself. But you will have to force yourself to let me in a little because I'm not going anywhere. I either take you home with me or we go on the scavenger hunt together. Your choice. What will it be?"

"You could leave me here," Bree said, her head down, looking at her cup.

"Can't. Won't," Cindy said. Looking at her friend, so thin her clothes hung on her, dark circles under her eyes, and hair that looked as if no one had noticed it for months, she added, "I can't let you go again, Bree. You look terrible. I was your best friend for years. We had a pact. You broke it.

"And now we are going to put it back together again whether or not you like it, because right now you are acting like a baby, and that's not the Bree that I know. We are going to bring Bree back. Maybe I'll have a t-shirt made that says, 'Bring Bree Back,' and sell it at my art gallery. That way, you will be embarrassed into action."

"You have an art gallery?" Bree said, looking up.

"That's what you got from that?" Cindy said. "Yes, I do. And Judith, April, and Marsha have had lives too. Lives you have missed. That changes now. The only question is, are you willing to do this, or do I have to drag you through it?"

Bree looked at Cindy and saw the little girl with long blond hair and bright blue eyes. The girl who had always been beside her, wanting to love her, needing to be loved back. It was both a weakness and a strength when they were growing up. But now, a woman stood in front of her, and that need was now a strength.

"Okay," Bree said.

Cindy, ready to keep arguing, had to stop herself from spouting more words, surprised by Bree's answer.

"Okay? That's all you have to say?"

"Yes, okay. But there are a few things to do first. I want to get this house ready to sell. I can't live here without Paul. That might take time."

"It won't. We'll call Judith. She'll get in touch with a realtor here and handle it all. We'll pack what you need to keep and put it into storage and ship it or come back for it later.

"In fact, if you are willing, you could give Judith a temporary power of attorney for you, and she can watch over all your interests. Whatever they are. Since none of us know exactly who you are anymore or what you do."

"Okay," Bree said again. The coffee was making her feel better. And Cindy taking over some of the decisions she was afraid to make lifted some of her anger and frustration. Besides, she knew that if she kept herself in a planning mode, she could keep the grief at bay. And they would be so busy Cindy might not ask her again why she and Paul had left. At least it would put off the question for now. It gave her time. Maybe Cindy would forget about it.

Bree knew that was a false hope. One of the pact would remember to ask. They'd ask over and over again until she told them or they figured it out. She kind of hoped they figured it out. It would relieve her of the responsibility of telling.

"But before we do anything, I need to get something done to my hair."

Cindy put her coffee down and started laughing. "OMG girl, do you ever. But first, could we go out to breakfast?"

"Okay," Bree said again, enjoying the briefness of the word. It was simple. It said she was willing.

"But it has to be where no one knows me."

A few hours later, the two women returned home. Bree's hair had been cut to fall softly around her face, having found a drop-in salon one town away. When the hairdresser had started to say something about the condition of Bree's hair, Cindy had given her a look and shook her head. Smiling, the hairdresser nodded that she understood.

Now, back home with enough groceries to last a few days, it was time to make a call that Bree dreaded. That Cindy was almost bursting with excitement only increased the dread. Cindy had set up the call while Bree was getting her hair cut.

Cindy set up Bree's computer on the kitchen table, the window that looked out into Bree's back garden highlighting both their faces, and started the call.

As each woman's face popped up on the screen, Bree gasped, and by the time all three of them were there, tears were running down her face. What she had been terrified about had come true. She still cared about them, and the pain she had felt when she disappeared from their lives rushed back.

Marsha, who had disappeared for her own reasons and who understood how it could happen, said what they were all thinking.

"It doesn't matter why you left Bree. We're here together now."

Fourteen

The next few days passed quickly. Neither Bree nor Cindy had time to think about anything other than getting the house ready to sell. Cindy helped Bree put all the furniture on local selling sites, and within days most of it was gone. The rest was picked up by the Salvation Army, including the beds, so the last night in the house, they were both sleeping in sleeping bags.

Bree had Cindy take all the photo albums to a local person who scanned them and put them on a thumb drive. Then, despite Cindy's protest, Bree burned the physical albums in the backyard fire pit, claiming she was dedicating her life to traveling light. Neither of them mentioned that perhaps that was a response to the emotional weight she was lugging around.

Bree traded both their cars in for a new one, part of her starting-over-again decision. She didn't want to remember trips with Paul in her old car, thinking it would only make her feel more grief. She wanted to make fresh memories.

It was only as they packed the car with what they would need on a trip that Cindy fully realized that Paul's scavenger hunt involved a road trip. She should have realized it before but hadn't thought it through. A road trip meant more than a few days following Paul's clues. How would she keep her business going if she were away for that long?

Private conversations with Judith assured her it would be okay. Janet and Mimi understood the business well, and if they needed help, Judith would be there for them. And Janet said they had a few friends who would help if they got swamped with orders.

"Besides," Judith reminded her, "You might find other artists to represent on your trip, or maybe even regain your inspiration to be one yourself."

Cindy looked away so that Judith wouldn't see the tears that idea brought, but she knew Judith was fully aware of them and chose not to comment.

Once Bree decided she was leaving, she was all business. She and Judith worked out everything that Judith would need to sell the house and manage her accounts while they were traveling.

During the business conversation with Judith, they both found out what Bree did for a living.

"You are R.B. Curtis?" Judith had asked. "The real R.B
. Curtis?"

"Who is R.B. Curtis?" Cindy asked, staring at both of them.

"Only a best-selling romance writer," Judith answered, staring at Bree as if she was seeing her for the first time.

"You, write romance?" Cindy asked. "You?"

"Yes, what's the big deal? People don't get shocked by people writing fantasy, Sci-Fi, or any other genre. They know the writer of those genres make-up what they are writing. It's their imagination. It's writing for cripe's sake. That's what fiction writers do. They make things up."

When neither Judith nor Cindy said anything, Bree added, "Okay, I know, I'm not what you think romance writers are like, but that's the point. No one is. I made it up! What part don't you understand about this? Romance—all fiction—all made up."

When neither woman answered her, Bree sighed. "Yes, I know you want to know why I didn't write using my name. Was I hiding that I sometimes write spicy romance? No. I was hiding in general. And since you already know that I was hiding, what's the big deal? And yes, I took my real first name of Rhoberta—yes, I never shared that—and Bree, and my maiden name, and put them together. I thought it was clever."

"Well, it was," Judith answered. "I wasn't disapproving. I am a huge fan. And don't look at me like that, Cindy. Lots of people read romance. And since you clearly don't, maybe you should start."

"Only if there are clues to what we are doing on this road trip in the books," Cindy laughed. "Otherwise, I'll stick with my fantasy, thank you!"

Bree huffed again. "It's all fantasy!"

When Judith and Cindy laughed at her exasperation with them, Bree joined in, adding, "And that could be true about everything!"

After that revelation, Bree felt more at ease with Cindy, and on their last night in the house, sleeping on the floor, they laughed and giggled like they did when they were in school. Neither woman brought up the pending journey or Paul and Bree's disappearance from their friends' lives for almost thirty years.

Cindy decided to let Bree tell her about those things as they traveled. After getting over the shock of needing to be away from her business for so long, Cindy realized that a road trip was something she always wanted to do. She just didn't want to travel on her own or for no reason. Paul's last gift provided a reason for doing something she had dreamed about doing.

It occurred to Cindy, not for the first or last time, that Paul had planned this for all of them, not just for his wife. And whatever secrets it revealed was okay with him because he wouldn't be around to deal with the consequences. And Cindy knew there would be consequences. There had to be. Hopefully, good ones, but she was not so naïve as to think that there wouldn't also be bad ones.

Which meant she wasn't so sure that Paul had been such a good guy after all. Perhaps this was simply a way to ease a guilty conscience. The question was, did Bree know about it, or was she going to discover something that would alter everything she had believed about Paul?

All these thoughts occurred to Cindy as she drifted off to sleep. Giggling helped, but it didn't answer questions or ease the worry.

Bree lay in the darkness long after Cindy fell asleep, her mind racing. She was going to be homeless. She would have nothing except her memories, and she was terrified that what they would find would rip those away from her, too.

Fifteen

E ver since they had all received a letter from Paul, April had felt uneasy. She didn't like feeling that way. She wanted things settled and comfortable. Knowable. It was one reason she had married so young. Well, at the time, it didn't feel young. She had felt grown-up and responsible. Or at least she had told herself that because it made her decision the right one.

She had met Ron Page in her second semester of community college on the first day of history class when they both headed to the same seat in the lecture hall. Front row, left aisle seat. She always chose that seat.

Being short was a decided disadvantage. If you wanted to see the teacher, you had to sit up front. Sitting at the end of a row meant she could swivel out of her chair and be up and out of the room without stumbling over people.

For a split second, transfixed by the sight of him, she had paused, then said, "This is my seat," and then covered her mouth, afraid she had been too forward.

"Of course it is," he said, as he moved to the chair beside her. "Do you mind if I sit here?"

April had not only not minded, she loved it. Mostly. Because it didn't take long before his nearness distracted her from what the teacher was saying. Later, Ron had confessed to the same feeling. He told her a year later when he had asked her to marry him as they had dinner at their favorite restaurant.

Ron explained he was leaving to finish his schooling at the university, and he wanted her to go with him. April had hesitated only for a split second, thinking of the four friends she would leave behind and the plans she had made for herself once she got through school.

But the idea of spending the rest of her life with Ron chased every fear away. Her friends had been happy for her. At least she believed they had been. They had all cried and hugged as she and Ron drove away—her looking back and waving, Ron's eyes on the road taking them to their future.

That's the way their life had been for almost thirty years. Ron led the way. After Ron finished his degree, they moved even further away when Ron took a job in Silver Lake. He loved it. It was exciting and fulfilling for him and provided for his family, which he had always said was his priority.

April, who had grown up with parents who were carefree and sometimes not careful about providing for her, was grateful that Ron had kept his promise always to protect and provide for her and the kids.

Although the plan had been to finish school with Ron, instead, she worked to make sure he got through school. After that, the idea of going to school didn't appeal to her. Besides, she had gotten pregnant with their first child almost immediately.

While the children grew up, April kept herself busy being a full-time mom, raising two children who grew up to be adventurers like their grandparents. One started traveling, rarely settling down.

The other married and moved to Canada, leaving her and Ron to make a new life for themselves. The only adventure they planned would be to travel to see their grandchild when he was born.

They still sat beside each other. Ron, careful and planning, was always on her left, as he had been that first day of history class. But now that the kids were grown, she had grown restless. April worried that maybe her parents' carefree nature had finally surfaced in her after all these years.

She pretended that wasn't true, that she wasn't restless, that she wasn't wondering about what she had missed in life. Then Paul's letter arrived.

Until that day, it had been easy to tell herself that her life was exactly what she had wanted. She had said to herself that she needed nothing more.

But the letter made her face the truth that she did want more. What that was, or how it would happen in their carefully planned life, was not something she had allowed herself to think about until she read the letter.

Now that her friends, the ones she barely knew anymore, were caught up in Paul's scavenger hunt, the fear that she had missed out on something in her life and now would miss out on the adventure the others were having was causing her stomach to hurt.

She wanted to take part, but how? Ron liked her by his side, not gallivanting all over the country, as he had said when she mentioned visiting Judith and Cindy in Spring Falls.

"It's hardly gallivanting," she had laughed, thinking at first he was joking.

When he scowled at her for laughing, she stopped, stepped back, and looked at the man she had been married to all these years. Physically, he looked almost the same, just aged to perfection. Why men aged to look better and women simply aged had never seemed fair to her.

Ron's slightly nerdy appearance had matured, only making him more attractive. His brown hair had turned gray, and he didn't wear glasses anymore. Yes, at fifty, he was a very handsome man.

He kept his promises to me, April thought. But then, seeing the look he was giving her, asked herself how had she not noticed that her parents had always visited them, and never the other way around?

Her parents had both passed away a few years earlier, and since they had moved to Florida not long after she and Ron moved away, she had flown down for both their funerals, Ron and the children at her side.

Which meant there had only been one time she had been to Spring Falls since the day she had looked back and waved at her friends, wiping tears from her eyes, turned forward to face the life she and Ron would make together.

It was for Bree and Paul's wedding, and she suspected now that had only happened because Ron didn't want her friends to know how he intended to run her life from that point on. They might have stopped her then—if she would have listened—which was doubtful.

No, Ron would not be happy about her decision to do more with her life now. And she would start with helping Bree. It was time to be in the front row again. This time, life would be the teacher.

If Ron wanted to be beside her, she would be grateful. But either way, she was ready for something different in life. What that would be, April didn't know. It surprised her that she was pleased with the idea. But she had glimpsed the girl she used to be, and that meant she could not turn back. That girl, older and wiser, would make the decisions from now on.

Sixteen

This is harder than I thought it would be, Marsha thought. She was standing in the middle of the floor of her dance studio and could see herself in the mirror. The barre cut through her reflection, splitting her in half. She thought it was a perfect symbol of how she felt.

Her feet were grounded in the life she had lived for these past years, and her head was looking forward to another life.

Well, not actually another life, Marsha muttered to herself.

She had no idea what she would do once she returned to Spring Falls. Judith, ever practical Judith, suggested opening a school where she could continue to teach dance and theater. But the thought of doing that again felt suffocating to Marsha.

Yes, theatre and dance had been almost her entire life. She had left everything behind to go to New York. Then she left New York to come to this town to hide away from her failures and teach others what she couldn't do herself.

And now she was slinking home, still feeling like a failure. Well, perhaps not a complete failure. After all, she had earned a living doing what she loved all these years, if not as someone famous, at least successful on a small scale.

Not successful in love, though, Marsha reminded herself.

Not that she hadn't tried. Because she thought she had to. Everyone had relationships. And she had boyfriends, but she always disappointed them somehow. Or they disappointed her. She hadn't cared much. Or at least that's what she told herself. And maybe it was true; she didn't care that she hadn't found someone to give her life away to.

Marsha knew that kind of thinking was part of the problem. She was always worried that whomever she counted on would disappoint her. And she liked her independence. But she knew that there was another reason, and that reason was not something she felt like sharing with anyone. She barely shared it with herself.

A knock at the door interrupted her thoughts. She knew it was the realtor coming for the keys. The sale of her home and business would happen without her being present. It was better that way. She wasn't sure she could handle it in person.

Everything not part of the house and studio had been sold or given away. All that she wanted to keep was in her car, ready for her to begin a new life. Spring Falls wasn't that far away, and yet she had never visited, never gone back to see her friends.

There was no more family, her mother having finally drunk herself to death. Marsha had not even returned for her funeral. She had sent money for a cremation.

There would be no grieving, Marsha had told herself. She didn't need a grave to go to see someone who had never been there for her. Although once she got home, Marsha knew she had to do something with her mother's ashes. They currently resided on a shelf at the funeral home, waiting for her to pick them up. She'd put it off as long as she could, like everything else she didn't want to think about.

Judith had offered to let Marsha stay with her once she got to town, until she got settled. That Judith, who could barely stand how Marsha lived, had made such an offer, had stunned her. Although she didn't let it show, she just turned Judith down, saying she would stay at the local Bed And Breakfast until she found a place to rent.

Marsha was sure that Judith was relieved, even though she had given a good impression of disappointment. And then Cindy had called and asked Marsha if she would mind staying at her house while she and Bree went off on their scavenger hunt. Marsha was reasonably sure that had been Judith's idea—always practical—but Cindy said it would help her know someone was in the house taking care of it while she was gone.

"Yes," Marsha had finally said, once she realized it solved her current state of homelessness. She could trust it. Her friends hadn't ever let her down. She was the one that had left and not looked back, or at least didn't go back. But before going back to Spring Falls, she wanted to take a brief road trip of her own.

Sliding into the front seat of her car, Marsha took one last look at a life that was now over, flipped on her turn signal, and pulled away, heading for home, where perhaps she would find what she was looking for. But Marsha doubted it. Not knowing what that was would make it hard to find.

Once the letter from Paul arrived, Grace went into action. She had her car serviced and hired another barista.

She told people she was feeling restless and wanted to go on a small road trip.

Although she was entirely aware of the reaction those words produced in each person, she didn't worry. She wouldn't be gone long, and nothing she did would affect her current life or the people in it.

All she had to do was deliver some information to someone. But she had to wait until the instructions arrived, telling her it was time to go.

Grace, a naturally curious busybody, or as they now called her, Mother Hen, couldn't wait to find out more and be part of another adventure.

In the same envelope that contained Paul's letter was a card from his attorney, with a note to contact him with her phone number, because he would be the one who would let her know when to leave.

She had talked briefly with his secretary and given her the number of her cell phone. But no amount of her tactful interrogation methods worked to get more information.

All she knew was that she would tell someone what she knew. This message would have sounded cryptic to anyone else, and they might wonder what she knew she was supposed to tell. But Grace knew exactly what Paul wanted her to share. Why now? Well, that part she didn't know. But she couldn't wait to find out.

The only thing that worried Grace was knowing what she had to say would be hard for at least one person to hear, although telling it now couldn't hurt Paul anymore. She had kept Paul's secret all these years to ensure he had a second chance. She always believed in second chances. Grace hoped Paul had used his wisely.

Seventeen

Almost at the exact moment that Marsha pulled away from her house heading north, Cindy and Bree did the same thing heading east. Cindy drove, leaving Bree free to look back at the home where she and Paul had spent their lives together.

Bree watched her house shrink in the distance, telling herself that she had done her best to rid herself of any ties to the place so that nothing would remain of her and Paul. It would be a memory frozen in time, with no power over her and the new life she would make for herself.

Except Bree knew she was lying to herself. This place would always pull her back, whether or not she lived there. The trees they had planted together would grow more beautiful each year. Their carefully planned garden would remind her of the hours they had spent together, making it better.

The garden had been her escape from hours of writing. Results from hours of gardening were something she could tangibly see. Not like words that went out into the world with no way to physically see their impact. A book was tangible in some ways, but not the same way a seed planted and tended to in all seasons was to her.

When she was writing, she lived in an invisible world of her own making. Gardening was visible, engaged all the senses, and gave back more than it took. Because, after all these years, Bree wasn't so sure that writing gave back what it took from her.

Moving away and making a new life would help her decide if writing was something she wanted to continue or not.

At least I could make a story out of it, Bree thought to herself, and then smiled at the idea, realizing that she was fooling herself, thinking she could stop writing. But if she wrote again, she would write something other than romance.

"Are you okay?" Cindy asked, glancing over at Bree. She could almost feel the sadness radiating off of her.

"Yes."

"Nothing you want to do before leaving town?"

"Well, maybe eat?"

"Just what I was thinking," Cindy said.

"Well then, why didn't you say so?" Bree asked, more snap in her voice than she meant there to be. It was the part of her she didn't like.

She always tried to make things perfect and became resentful when they weren't. Bree knew that wasn't really who she was, just behavior she could eliminate, and over the years, she had worked hard at doing that, Paul didn't like that part of her any more than she did.

But he wasn't perfect either, Bree said to herself. Never out loud. Not then, not now.

When Cindy didn't answer, just looked away for a second, Bree added, "Sorry."

"Don't fret about it," Cindy answered, turning to smile at Bree. "Where shall we eat?"

"The Waffle House," they both said together and then laughed, for the moment wiping away Bree's past and her pain.

An hour later, two pecan waffles later, they were on the road, Bree driving this time, the map to where they were going showing on the car's GPS. It was the first time that Cindy knew where they were going.

"That's where we are going?" she asked.

"Yep."

"What was the clue?"

Bree sighed. Perhaps she should have shown Cindy the letter rather than keeping it to herself. But for now, Bree was trying to keep Paul's memory pure, as if that was possible.

While they were together, she hadn't noticed how much she had changed. But Paul's letter had made her look at everything in a new light.

Yes, in the letter he told her he loved her, always loved her, always would love her. And then he apologized for taking her away.

She had stopped reading the letter at that point, gone into the kitchen, made a cup of coffee, and tried to stop her mind from racing. Yes, Paul had taken her away. But not because he wanted to. It was her idea, and he did what she asked.

What kind of idiot had she been? She had given up her friends and the life she thought she wanted to live because she had a secret, and he agreed to protect it.

At least that was what she thought had happened.

But Paul's apology in the letter made her question her memory. Why was he so agreeable about keeping her secret? Was her secret the only one they were protecting? Did he have one too?

Bree had believed that Paul had given up on the life he wanted because of her. But what if that wasn't the entire truth? What if her insistence on hiding suited him? Maybe he kept her secret because he had one too.

All those thoughts raced through her mind as she drank her coffee. It took a few hours before she returned to the letter, finally reading Paul's request that she go on a type of scavenger hunt with one or more of her friends from Spring Falls. It was his last gift to her.

"The trip will do you good," the letter said. "And along the way, you'll find yourself again.

"My only hope," he had closed with, "is that you don't hate me for what you find."

That last line was the line that tore her heart apart. The fear of what it meant had kept her silent. What would she find? Would she end up hating him? Was he not who she thought he was? Did they leave Spring Falls for a reason other than to protect her secret?

She almost tore up the letter. Instead, she kept it, reading it over and over again, and in the process realized that her heart had been closed for many years, thinking it kept her safe. From what, she didn't know, but obviously, that had worked. Perhaps their life had been an illusion.

What Bree decided was that it was time to breathe again. To do what Paul asked of her and get on with it.

Cindy waited, watching Bree breathe in and out, knowing that she was reliving a decision.

Finally, Bree sighed again and said, "There was no clue. He just told me to start where we had stopped."

"Sounds like a clue to me?" Cindy said. "Stopped when?"

"We took a road trip once. I was restless. Paul was between jobs. It seemed like a good idea. And it was. Both of us loved that trip. That last day we stopped at a rest stop, and Paul asked me if I would like to keep on driving east.

"Part of me wanted to say yes. Perhaps we could travel forever, never settling down. But I said no. It was time to return to real life, whatever I thought that was.

"Now, looking back, I realize he wanted me to say yes. I don't know why, and I don't know what we will find there, but I know that is where he wants me to begin."

Eighteen

Nothing in Bree's books helped Judith. There were no clues to Bree's real world in her writing. The storyline of boy and girl meet, fall in love, get pulled apart, and come together, in the end, was standard for the genre.

There was no hint of why Bree and Paul had left Spring Falls and why Paul wrote them all a letter and begged them to take Bree on a scavenger hunt after his death.

Perhaps the attorney can shed some light on these questions, Judith thought. Anything would help, because at this point, she was on her own.

April had been uncharacteristically quiet since the first Zoom call together. It was almost as if she wished she had never heard about Paul and Bree and the letters. Bree and Cindy had started their trip, heading to a rest stop on route 86 in New York State.

Marsha had called and said she had changed her mind. She wouldn't be coming straight to Spring Falls. Could Judith look after Cindy's house instead? Marsha explained that hearing about Bree and Cindy's trip had sparked a desire to take a journey of her own.

Marsha said she needed time to think and adjust to what she was doing. She had a place in mind that she always wanted to see in lower New York State. She'd start there and see where her whims took her next.

The thought that Cindy, Bree, and Marsha were all traveling in New York and that there was a tiny chance they would meet, or at least pass each other, flashed through Judith's mind.

She supposed she could make it happen by telling them all they were in the same general vicinity. But decided not to. At least for the moment. If she were going to meddle with what was going on, she would start with the attorney.

Since Cindy wasn't in town, there was no point in having coffee in the coffee shop. Instead, she made her own, took out one of the cinnamon buns she had stashed in the freezer after her last baking spree, and headed to the office.

Besides reading romance novels, Judith baked to take her mind off work. In sprees. If she was stuck on a problem, or someone was driving her crazy more than usual, she'd take the afternoon, sometimes a whole day, and bake things to eat that no one should eat, but everyone did.

She'd take a sampler to the office for clients and her roster of independent bookkeepers and accountants that did most of the grunt work in her business. Then she would freeze the rest, so there were always goodies in the freezer for days like this.

Today she needed an extra dose of courage because something told her that once she started digging around in Paul's life, which she intended to do, she'd discover something that Bree would not like. That is, if she didn't already know about it. Either way, the place to begin was with Paul's attorney, Mr. Bruce Dawson.

• • • ● ● • ● • • •

He had expected that eventually, someone would call him. Judith's phone call and her questions were easy to deflect, but he knew that wouldn't be the case next time.

The question he had been wrestling with ever since Paul had handed him the letters to mail after he died was how much he would tell. It would be a straightforward answer if Paul hadn't waived his attorney-client privilege because then he could claim that he couldn't tell them anything.

But Paul had put him in the position of making a choice himself. He hadn't liked it when Paul had done that, and he liked it even less now that Paul was gone because he couldn't argue with him anymore. How much would he tell? How much did they need to know? He had decided to continue to claim he couldn't tell what he knew unless someone was in danger.

Bruce Dawson swore under his breath at Paul, hoping that Paul was somewhere he could hear him. When Paul was alive, he was just a client he barely knew. They had met in college but hadn't hung out together for years, so it surprised him when he got the phone call.

"Why me?" he had asked Paul.

"Because I know you are trustworthy."

Bruce wasn't sure how Paul knew that, but he knew that was his intention.

They had greeted each other as old friends, even though they had not been that close. But it was good to see someone from his younger days. However, once they had spent a few minutes catching up, Bruce switched into an attorney mode and asked Paul only the questions he needed to know legally.

Paul resisted. And now, after Paul's death, he was stuck with this extra baloney Paul had asked him to do. He didn't feel happy about it. And now he had that woman, Judith, on his case.

His phone dinged, telling him it was time to log onto the Zoom link that Judith had sent him. He didn't want to do a Zoom call. A phone call would be so much better.

It was easier to dodge questions, easier to stonewall. But then this Judith person probably knew that. He had agreed because he knew that eventually, he would be swept up into Paul's plan. He might as well get it over with.

He swore at Paul again, muttering, "Why didn't you just tell them, buddy?" and logged into the call.

At first, all he saw was the back of her head, but when he said hello, she swiveled around to face him.

"Oh," she said.

That was one more word than Bruce could say.

For a fleeting second, Judith went back to the day that Bree had told them all, "That's the man I am going to marry."

She had thought it was ridiculous. How could you know with one look?

That Bree and Paul had married hadn't changed her mind. It was random. Bree had made a simple attraction to a stranger into what she wanted it to be and then made it work.

The two of them stared at each other before Bruce cleared his throat and asked, "You have questions?"

All Judith could think was, do I ever, before clearing her own throat and saying the stupidest thing ever, "You are Bruce Dawson, Paul Mann's attorney?"

For the first time since Paul had come to see him, Bruce was happy to answer, "Yes, yes, I am."

Nineteen

"This is it," Bree said, pulling into the parking lot of the Chautauqua Lake Rest area.

"The clue is here?" Cindy asked, wondering how that could be true.

Bree shrugged, trying not to let her face show any emotion. It was hard to be here remembering the last time with Paul.

Besides, she thought, *I could be wrong about the whole thing. The clue might not be here at all.* So she said nothing, just pointed the way to the bathrooms.

Afterward, Bree stayed in the lobby looking at maps and information while Cindy stepped outside to see the view. Bree joined her a few minutes later, still not saying anything.

"This is it? Really?" Cindy finally asked again. "It's stunning, but where is the clue?"

They had been standing near a low stone wall, looking out over the view for the last twenty minutes. Not moving, not talking.

Finally, Bree turned to look at Cindy, and Cindy was happy to see that there was more color in Bree's face, and although there were tears in her eyes, she seemed more at peace.

"It's beautiful, isn't it?" Bree asked.

"Stunning," Cindy answered.

From where they were standing, they could see for miles. A large green lawn lay behind them, and Chautauqua Lake stretched out before them. The entire scene radiated peace.

Perhaps a legacy from Indian tribes who had once lived in these spaces, Cindy thought.

Still looking out over the lake, Bree sighed as if deciding what to say.

"It's hard to believe that it's been twenty years since we took that road trip. I have so many memories of it, but mostly I remember how happy I was that we were together.

"Just us, looking at things we had never seen before. I would wish for an Internet connection when we camped or stayed at motels, but they weren't always available then.

"It was such a short time ago, and yet everything was different. We wanted to take pictures and keep them on our computer. It sounds normal now, but then it was a new idea. There were no cell phones with their fantastic cameras.

"We've always been first adopters, so we bought a new-fangled camera with floppy disks. We could fit maybe five or ten pictures on each disk. I would download them off the disks and put them on my computer. Everyone thought it was the coolest thing ever.

"Now, we have GPS in our phones and cars, but then we didn't. Instead, Paul and I had this small yellow plastic box from Delorme that we stuck on the car's front window.

"There weren't many satellites for it to see then, and sometimes it would blink out, but to us, it was magic. We had a swivel stand mounted in front of the passenger seat where we put my computer, which was attached to the yellow box with a long cord, and that's how we saw where we were.

"Sometimes I would write as we drove. But mostly, I watched the computer screen and told Paul where we were and what road to take.

"Every time we'd pull into some public place, and I would slide out of the car, people would stare at the setup. We enjoyed making people wonder what it was. Sometimes they asked, usually they just stared.

"Because there were few satellites, sometimes we got lost anyway, but that was part of the fun. Triple-A was part of that system, and we could look at what was around us using their program. Once in a while, we'd take a detour to see something, and other times, I would read the history of the town and the areas we were passing through to Paul.

"Ever since that trip, when we saw something on a movie or TV show, we'd love to say 'we've been there!' We relived that trip repeatedly in so many ways."

Cindy waited for Bree to say more, but instead, she walked across the lawn to the patio and took a seat. Cindy followed, not saying anything, waiting, knowing there must be more, but when Bree stayed silent, Cindy finally asked, "What prompted you to take the trip?"

"Me. I was stuck on a book I was writing, and I was probably not pleasant to be around. Paul asked what he could do, and I said I didn't know. But I felt as if I was trapped.

"The next day, Paul told me he arranged to take the entire summer off so we could go on a road trip. He said he had accumulated vacation time. I didn't understand how he could take all that time off, but then I didn't understand what he did at work, so I just went with it. The idea of a road trip was so appealing I only asked how soon we could leave.

"It was the perfect solution to how I felt. I don't know how Paul knew. He wasn't the greatest at understanding feelings, but right then, he did. And I loved him even more for that."

"So you traveled all over the country that summer?"

"We did," Bree answered, smiling at the memory.

"And yet, you didn't come to see any of us. You'd been gone for years. We didn't know where you lived or why you left. You could have at least stopped by and said hello."

The moments stretched out before them. Bree could imagine her past lying before them on the surface of the lake, almost within reach before it sank out of sight.

The trouble was, she thought, *the past doesn't stay out of sight. It always floats back to the surface.*

"Couldn't," she finally answered.

"Couldn't or wouldn't?" Cindy asked, trying not to let the hurt of feeling unwanted affect her voice. It was enough that she had cried almost every night for that first year when Bree left. That was enough crying.

"Both," Bree said.

Turning to Cindy, she took both her hands before saying, "I wish I had enough courage to tell you then, and I wish I had it now. But I am here on this trip with you, hoping to find out the truth about myself and Paul, and maybe that will give me that courage to be the friend you deserve."

Tears gathered in Cindy's eyes, and she nodded, not trusting herself to say anything.

A blast of wind and rumble of thunder startled them both.

"If I were younger, I would say 'race you to the building!'" Cindy said, laughing as the first drops of rain began to fall.

A few minutes later, Bree and Cindy joined the other travelers, who had also been out walking or looking at the view of the large

Victorian building that was both incongruous and delightful as a rest stop.

While they waited out the storm, they ate snacks from the vending machine and chatted about nothing.

"It's almost like being back in school eating out of vending machines," Cindy said, licking the last of the salt from her bag of chips off of her fingers.

Bree nodded, "Except for all the little kids and all the old people like us, and teenagers who look as if they would rather not be here. Yep, just like then."

Seeing the hurt on her friend's face, she added, "Thank you for coming, Cindy. Not sure if I said that yet."

"Truthfully, I realize I need this as much as you. Where to next? Was there a clue here?"

"I didn't think there was until a moment ago when I remembered what Paul said while we were here. It could be nothing, and I don't know how he could think that I would remember.

"But then, Paul knows—knew—me well. He would have known I would wait for an idea or a memory to come back, and thanks to the storm and pausing to eat, it did."

Cindy made a hurry-up gesture with her hand, and Bree laughed.

Pointing at one of the maps mounted on the wall, she said, "We were standing in front of that map, and he pointed to a place on it and said, 'That's where it all began.'"

Twenty

Cindy reached across the table and touched Bree's hand. Looking at her friend's face, she couldn't tell how Bree felt. That was nothing new. She was well aware of Bree's internal walls and how she disappeared inside her thoughts. But right now, she needed Bree to stop being such a loner and share.

"Did you just leave it at that? You couldn't have. I know you, Bree. You are always trying to solve things to find out the truth behind stories. What happened next?"

This is the moment, Bree thought. *Either go forward and find out what he meant, or go home. Wherever that is now.*

Looking across the table at her friend Cindy waiting patiently as she always had, she wanted to get up and run out of the rest stop. Cindy could call Judith, and she'd find a way to get her home.

She could disappear again. Write under another name. Maybe forget spicy romance. Write detective stories, instead. It would be so easy, just as it had been thirty years before.

The problem is, Bree thought, *I'm awake now.* And mad, she realized. Mad at herself, mad at Paul and his stupid secrets. Mad because she had thought love would be enough. Well, it wasn't. Paul left her.

It's time to get my life back, Bree said to herself. *I've run away for too long.*

Taking a deep breath and slowly releasing it, Bree smiled at her friend and said, "I asked him, What began? But he refused to say more. So what, I thought. Paul has secrets. I told myself that I didn't mind as long as we were together.

"But now, I realize I should have asked more questions. I think I was afraid it would break our life open, and awful things would spill out. Things we had put in there together, and things we had packed away from each other. Maybe he wanted to tell me then and would have told me if I had asked what he meant."

"That's on him, Bree, not you. But if you're right, he must have wanted you to know now. In this strangely weird way, he is giving you the answers he couldn't give you then. Otherwise, why write the letters? Why send us on this trip? No matter what happens, our pact will be by your side through this whole thing."

When Bree turned away, her face flushed, Cindy guessed what she was thinking, "And yes, even after we find out why you left, we'll be here."

"Are you sure about that?" Bree whispered. How would they forgive her for what she had done?

"Positive! So what, or where, did he point to?"

Bree took another deep breath before answering, knowing it was the beginning of the end, and once she started, there would be no stopping.

"I only remember where he pointed because I asked him what he meant. He said it was nothing, just that his life had been the pits since his parents died, just like the town. His face turned hard, and I was scared for a minute. I had never seen him that upset. He wasn't one to show his emotions, so I wasn't sure what he was feeling, just that it wasn't a good thing.

"I stayed silent, afraid he'd erupt into some emotion I couldn't handle. When I said nothing, he gave me a tiny smile and said, 'give me a minute' and then went outside to the stone wall.

"After he stepped away, I looked at the map, and where I thought he had pointed, I saw there was a town called Pittsfield in Massachusetts."

"That's a stretch, isn't it? Besides, you said he mumbled. And you don't know for sure that he pointed to the town called Pittsfield at all."

"No, I don't, but I am sure enough to try it. Besides, it's in the Berkshires, and if you've never been there, it's worth the trip."

"Even if we don't find anything?"

"Even if, but I think we will. I need to find out what Paul meant when he said it all began there. What began there? Paul never told me anything about his past life. At least not enough to piece anything together."

"So, leaving places and people was something Paul was doing before you met him?"

"Appears that way," Bree answered, standing up and rattling her keys.

"So this is not connected to why you left us?"

Bree gave Cindy a long look, slung her purse over her shoulder, squared her shoulders, and turned away.

Just when Cindy thought she would say nothing more, Bree turned back and said, "I don't know. Let's find out, shall we?"

Twenty-One

Marsha read Cindy's text and slapped the wheel of her car in astonishment. How likely was it that the three of them were moving in the same direction? Well, not moving in the same direction. Headed in the same direction.

She was traveling north, and they were coming from the west. She hadn't intended to go to Pittsfield, Massachusetts. Why would she? Instead, she had driven up the Taconic State Parkway to see the sculpture gardens.

Long ago, she had driven this road and seen the huge concrete head above the ridge overlooking the parkway and wondered what it was. When she decided to take a brief road trip to clear her head first before returning to Spring Falls she thought of that head and decided it was time to find out what it was and then see it for herself.

Marsha discovered that the sculpted head was completed in 1996 by self-taught sculptor Roy Kanwit. She learned that the head represents Gaea, the Greek Mother Earth, and because it's hollow, people can climb through a hole in the top of it and take in her stunning view of the surrounding Hudson River Valley, mountains, and river.

When Marsha learned that there were thirty more massive statues, all inspired by various mythologies—including Egyptian, Native American, Greek, and Roman—in that sculpture garden, it cemented her determination to go.

She needed to move out into the world. She had fallen into a rut in life. It was time to get out. Perhaps the massive statues would help release her from the small safe place she had built within herself.

And when she read that the sculptor was self-taught, she hoped that seeing his work might help dissolve some of her beliefs that she had to know how to do things before actually doing them. Instead, maybe she could begin and let that tell her what she wanted to do for the rest of her life. What that was, she didn't know yet. She hoped the trip would reveal it to her.

Marsha knew that Cindy and Bree were further away from Pittsfield than she was, so she had time to stop and see the park first. Besides, the parkway was beautiful, and because it was only open to passenger vehicles, there was no driving with trucks, which would have spoiled the experience. The parkway was designed so a driver could take in the beauty of its surroundings. That's what she wanted in her life—beauty. That's what she thought dance would bring her. And it did. Briefly. And then it didn't.

She thought it ironic that they were heading to a town called Pittsfield. Pits Ville was the space in her head where she had been living so long she almost forgot there was someplace else. Marsha was sure that the town wasn't called Pittsfield because it was the pits. Even so, that's where the name took her.

Marsha texted Judith, telling her where she was and that she too would head to Pittsfield and meet Cindy and Bree there, but she wanted to surprise them.

Judith wrote back and asked if that was a good idea?

"Yes, it is," Marsha replied.

In response, Judith just texted a row of hearts, showing support and keeping her opinions to herself. Marsha understood the question, even though she had pretended not to.

Although she had moved away from Spring Falls and the pact too, Bree's leaving and then refusing to be found had broken her heart, too. Not that she would say that out loud, but, of course, Judith knew. Judith was worried that their meeting would not be the heartwarming meeting that perhaps Marsha imagined.

Or maybe she didn't imagine that at all. Perhaps she was thinking of a confrontation between the two of them. Because, being truthful with herself, she knew she was still angry and bitter about being on her own.

It didn't matter that she had chosen that path for herself. She had picked it with very little fear because she thought Bree would always be near and would support her and encourage her to go forward. She would come to New York to see her in a show, and they would celebrate together.

None of that happened. Her best friend abandoned her. Yes, she abandoned the entire pact, too, but that didn't mean it hurt less. Marsha knew that buried in her head was the thought that perhaps she would have succeeded after all if Bree had been in her life, to remind her of what she wanted and pick her up when she fell.

Yes, she knew it wasn't fair to make her failure to reach her dream of stardom partially Bree's fault. But it turned out that Bree had been just like her mother. No, not a drunk. But someone who was there one minute and gone the next. Because it had been her life, that fear had kept her from having any lasting relationship. She would break off all relations before they left her, which, of course, is what they would do given enough time.

99

After Bree's disappearance, it was what she had done with the pact too. She had broken it off, so they couldn't abandon her first. And now she wanted back in. Marsha understood that Judith and Cindy had never seen her outside the pact. Instead, they had just patiently waited for her to circle back around to them. But Bree and April had lived separate lives, and Marsha didn't believe she had been included in their thoughts at all.

So yes, there was a danger that instead of hugging and making up when she saw Bree, she would explode in frustration and pent-up anger. But she couldn't keep putting off the meeting, and in this way, it would be on her terms. Besides, if she were going to explode, perhaps it would be best to do it far from home. And strangers could be witnesses to what happens when people keep secrets and leave their best friends behind.

In the distance, Marsha could see the concrete head watching over the parkway. The voice on her GPS told her to take the next exit just a few miles ahead. Now that she had a destination, Marsha realized how much she had missed the process of setting out to someplace new, not knowing what would happen. She used to have courage. It was time to return to herself, and that giant Gaia head would be the first stop on that journey.

Twenty-Two

April stood beside her kitchen sink, surveying the mess on the floor, so stunned she couldn't move. But then, as the adrenaline that had surged began to fade, she started to shake and slid to the floor, hugging her knees to make herself as small as possible.

The sharp smell of the relish that had spilled out of its broken jar, mixed with the tang of mustard and hot sauce, made her feel slightly nauseous. April thought the green, red, and brown looked like a painting as she tried to make sense of what she was looking at.

The oat milk container had popped its lid and was slowly spreading into the mix of ingredients that used to be in her refrigerator and now lay on the floor.

It was the oat milk that had stopped the throwing. It was probably because instead of a satisfying crash and shatter, it just thunked, lay there, and then began leaking.

A part of April's brain saw the whole thing as a metaphor. Her life had been in cold storage in the refrigerator, and Ron had done her a favor and thrown it all at her, revealing something she had not known before. Now it was leaking, and there was no way to put it back.

For an hour, April sat on the floor, reliving what had happened and not understanding why it had. All she knew was she needed to clean up this mess, both the mess of the floor and the mess in her life. The one April didn't know she had until at 7:01 a.m. when she had casually told Ron she was going to visit Judith, and the pact was going to all be there. Did he want to come with her?

She had her back turned to Ron as she said it, buttering his toast for breakfast, not thinking anything about it. Sure, he hadn't seemed very happy about the letter from Paul, even though it had said nothing other than asking them all to help Bree when the time came. But he must have known she had kept in touch with Judith all this time.

Or did he, she asked herself now as the oak milk slowly edged towards her feet. Had she not told him? And if she hadn't, why not? Had she always known he wouldn't be happy about it and had kept that part of her life separate? Why would she have done that?

After all, he had been Paul's best man. They had all known each other back then. And it wasn't Ron's fault that Paul and Bree had moved away and never spoke to them again. Was this why he had reacted how he had?

April shuddered, remembering Ron's response when she told him her plans. First, it was a quiet "no."

Still not understanding, she turned with the toast in her hands and casually asked, "No? Why not?"

Ron had looked up at her, his brown eyes so dark they looked almost black, his usually handsome face now hard, his lips thinned, and April had stepped back, still holding the plate of toast.

Ron stood, his chair falling over as he did so, and she dropped the plate in shock, the toast landing butter side down on their newly installed cork floor, and she idly wondered if the butter would stain the floor.

Now looking at the relish, the mustard, hot sauce, and oak milk spreading out before her, April laughed hysterically. She had been worried about butter on the floor—now look.

When the plate landed on the floor, Ron had started towards her, fist raised, and she had stared at him as if she had never seen him before. Never in all their years together had she seen this Ron. It was as if a switch had gone off in him. But instead of hitting her, he had turned to the refrigerator and started throwing things.

Until the oak milk thunked, and that had stopped him.

"No. I forbid it," Ron said and walked out of the room, the front door slamming behind him, leaving her with a mess to clean up.

When the milk reached her bare feet, April realized she needed to move. Away from this mess. And she needed help.

She stood and edged her way over to her mobile phone that was charging at the end of the counter and face-timed the only friend she had she could trust. And it was that realization that took her over the edge. She didn't have friends. Not the kind you could trust. Just Judith, and maybe the pact. Shaking so hard she could barely talk, she said the only word that could come out.

"Help."

Seeing April's white face, Judith felt both terror and anger rising in her as she asked, "Honey, what's wrong?"

April turned her phone to the mess on the floor, and Judith gasped.

"What happened?"

"Ron."

"What do you mean, Ron?" Judith asked while a part of her brain registered all the years that April and Ron had never visited and how secretive April had been about calling her.

April always called when Ron wasn't around. Judith had seen possessive husbands before, and she accepted that April had married someone like that. But April had seemed contented and happy. Today she was terrified.

"I told him I was coming to Spring Falls to see the pact, and he said no. When I asked why, this was his response."

"Where is he now?"

"Work?" April responded, realizing she didn't know. Ron had been a good husband and father. Her life had been satisfying, and she had been happy, she thought. What had she missed?

"April, listen to me. Pack a bag, get in your car, and come here now."

April glanced at the mess on the floor.

"I know you, April. You're going to want to clean up that mess. Just throw some towels over it if you must, but get out. The floor can be replaced, but you can't."

"But, Ron..." April stuttered, realizing that her life as she knew it might be over.

"But, Ron, nothing! He can come here and explain to all of us why he did that. And if he can't, well, you have children to go to, and you have us."

When April hadn't moved, Judith lowered her voice and said, "Listen, I'm going to tell you what to bring. I'll stay on the phone until you are in the car and heading this way. Okay?"

April nodded.

"Okay, take that charger, bring your phone. Let's go to your bedroom so you can get a few clothes."

When April still hadn't moved, Judith said, "Now April! Follow my voice. You can do it."

Gathering all her strength, April pulled the charger out of the wall, walked out of the kitchen away from the mess, and headed into the bedroom. She didn't look at anything other than what Judith told her to look at.

April gathered clothes, makeup, and toiletries from the bathroom. She put them all into Ron's suitcase, realizing for the first time that she didn't have one of her own, bumped it down the steps, heaved it into the car, and drove out of town, Judith still on the phone, encouraging and promising that everything would be okay.

April doubted that, but she had to believe in something, and old friends seemed like the best place to begin.

Twenty-Three

J udith hung up, finally sure that April was safe and on her way and would not turn around and go back. She was exhausted from dealing with the attorney, Bruce, and now April and Ron acting crazy.

No, she corrected herself. It was first the letter, then Marsha, then her best friend, Cindy, off on the adventure with Bree. All of them left her here to deal with it all.

What you need is a good meal, Judith said to herself. *At your favorite restaurant,* she added.

She knew which one that was. The restaurant where she took her clients when she wanted to give them a treat. Today she would give herself a treat.

Judith decided to walk to the restaurant instead of driving. It would give her a chance to think through what was happening. Before Paul's letter arrived, she and Cindy had settled into a nice routine.

After the pact dispersed, the only two left in town, they did their best to keep it going. She and April would talk every few weeks, and they both had followed Marsha on social media, so they knew what she was doing, but it wasn't reciprocal. And, of course, Bree had disappeared.

She and Cindy kept her memory alive as best they could, celebrating her birthday every year, but without her. Actually, except for the two of them, they celebrated everyone's birthday that way, without the birthday girl.

Judith thought about texting Cindy what was happening with April but then decided not to. She would have enough to deal with when Marsha surprised her in Pittsfield. She still wasn't sure that was a good idea, but sometimes it was best to let things work themselves out.

Not in April's case, Judith thought to herself. Not when someone throws things and tries to own people. No. Not on her watch. She did not know what was going on with Ron, but she'd find out and do whatever she needed to do to fix it.

Judith didn't realize it—she was so busy with her thoughts—but as she walked, she talked to herself.

Everyone knew Judith, and as they watched her stride down the sidewalk, they shook their heads. That was Judith. Something was up that bothered her, and she was going to fix it.

They all loved her for it, but were also somewhat afraid. What if she had discovered something they had done that didn't sit well with Judith? You never knew. She was always looking for what didn't work or didn't feel right.

So they stepped out of her way and felt a sense of relief that she wasn't heading towards them. And also gratitude that Judith was out to right some kind of wrong somewhere, as long as it wasn't with them.

By the time Judith reached ParaTi's, she had worn herself out thinking, so when she opened the door, she was grateful that she had arrived. She didn't have to ask for her favorite table. The hostess took her straight back to the table in the corner where she could observe the room, but not be observed herself.

Like most of the businesses in town, ParaTi's finances were in her capable hands, and they were grateful for it and treated her with respect and kindness, with a small amount of fear that somehow they had done something wrong.

Many of the young people in town called the restaurant Party, and Judith knew the owner didn't mind. When they first met, the owner had told Judith that the name meant 'for you' in Spanish, so whatever people wanted to call it was alright with her, as long as they came by to eat.

"Beautiful day," the hostess said as she handed her the menu, and Judith smiled up at her in response, just in time to see her favorite waitress heading her way.

Mary Patterson had arrived in town the year before with her fiance, Seth Patterson, and immediately found a job at ParaTi. She and Judith had hit it off right away. Judith, ever curious, always inquired about how things were with the new waitress, and eventually, Mary had told her most of her life story. When Mary and Seth married six months ago, both Cindy and Judith had attended her wedding.

The last time Judith was at the restaurant, Mary had confided to her she was pregnant and both delighted and worried. She worried because they struggled now to make ends meet. How would they do it with a baby? But delighted because being a mother was something she had yearned for since she was a young girl.

After learning about Mary's pregnancy, Judith and Cindy discussed how they could help Mary. They already left generous tips, which Mary had first tried to turn away, but had finally yielded and now graciously accepted them.

Although Judith usually only saw Mary at the restaurant, Judith treasured the friendship. It was another reason she loved this small town and why she stayed. She also had to admit she enjoyed being a big fish in a small pond. Plus, everyone thought they knew her already, which suited her perfectly.

"Your usual, Judith?" Mary asked.

"Yes, please. How are you feeling? Do you have a due date yet?"

"Much better. Those first two months were rough. October 13th is the estimated time of arrival!"

"May Cindy and I give you a baby shower once it gets closer?"

Judith watched Mary's eyes fill with tears, and Mary looked away for a moment before nodding yes. Judith knew Mary didn't have parents who could do that for her. Or at least, not parents that Mary knew about.

Mary had confided to Judith that she was adopted. It wasn't something she had known her whole life, although she had suspected. Her mother had told her just before she passed away unexpectedly, apologizing for not telling her before, but she waited too long and didn't want to ruin their relationship.

All Mary could do was forgive her mom and thank her for raising her. She didn't want to spoil what they had or make her mother feel bad. Mary understood that her mother had done something out of love. So she didn't force her to tell her who her parents were. She asked just once, and her mom had said it was best not to know.

Mary said it was a mystery she wasn't interested in solving when Judith offered to help her find out. Judith had immediately disagreed, but she stayed silent out of respect for Mary's love for her adopted mother. But not knowing things always made a mess in the end, at least in Judith's opinion. However, she told herself to stay out of it. It was Mary's life, and she could choose.

By the time Judith had finished her pasta primavera and drunk two glasses of iced tea, she felt much better. She had made a list on her phone of things she needed to do to help the other members of the pact and a few ideas about what they could do to help Mary with the new baby.

But first, she had clients to attend to, and then she could deal with what Bruce had told her, or more accurately, not told her. She chose to stuff away the memory of what happened when she first saw him. She couldn't deal with whatever that was right now. There were bigger issues to take care of, and her feelings was not one of them.

Twenty-Four

G race knew that patience was a virtue, but she wasn't sure she had much of that. It had been a few weeks since she had received Paul's letter, and every day she was on high alert, waiting for his lawyer to tell her when she was supposed to leave.

She would return to a town she never thought she would see again. She had almost forgotten what had happened there. Almost.

Grace was well aware of the connections and strings that pulled people together. Most of those connections were invisible to almost everyone, even to her, but she trusted that was how the universe works, and she knew something, and it was time to tell it.

And now, because Paul's lawyer had her contact information, and she had her replacements in place at her coffee shop, she didn't have to stay and wait for the message. She could take herself off on a personal adventure.

She'd have to assure her friends she was fully capable of traveling on her own, and Grace knew a few of them might use their "magical" gifts of remote viewing to make sure she was okay, but the point was, she didn't have to wait.

Grace had always wanted to visit Frank Lloyd Wright's Falling Water, and it wasn't that far from where she lived. She'd start there. Then, if Paul's lawyer hadn't contacted her yet, she'd find something else to see. She'd stay close, so she would always be just a day's drive away from where she had to go and could head there once she got the message that it was time.

The more Grace thought about it, the more she liked the idea. It would give her a break between Doveland and meeting Paul's widow and time to collect herself before telling her what she knew. Grace knew it wouldn't be easy to hear and almost as hard to tell. But then, almost fifty years had passed. Perhaps it wasn't as vital as she kept making it out to be.

Grace sighed as she thought about the past. Years ago, when this thing with Paul had happened, she had been more naïve and much less aware of the ramifications of decisions, and she wondered now if she had made the right one then.

Bruce Dawson logged out of the call with Judith and swiveled his chair away from the computer. As if that would change what had happened.

From his desk, Bruce's view was a huge apple tree that was now blooming outside his window and was so close he felt as if he was living in it.

Bruce could see that overnight the tree had sprouted a burst of green leaves, replacing some blossoms that were now drifting past his window. The branches waved back and forth in the breeze, bathing the room in filtered light.

He loved all the seasons of the tree. Spring with closed buds one day and bursting open the next, the summer green, fall apples, and winter when the tree stood bare against the often gray sky. Everything about the tree pleased him.

Bruce spent many hours watching the birds that nested in it and the bees that moved from flower to flower doing their work. He loved witnessing how the tree and bees worked together to keep the planet alive, and wished people could be more like birds, trees, and bees.

When he arrived that morning, Bruce had opened the window to let in the light breeze. Now he could smell the apple blossoms and lilacs that grew in the corner of the small garden in the back of the building. The gardener had brought up an armful of lilacs to his secretary, and she had them on her desk, so the smell of spring was everywhere.

Bruce considered the tree and the bees the perfect symbol of how life was supposed to work. Freely giving, flowing with life, and working in tandem and community. Seeing how they worked together kept his drive to do things his way in check. Or at least kept it from running amuck. He told no one, but if he was having trouble deciding what the right thing to do was, he'd ask himself if the tree and the bees would approve of his decision.

It was probably not what people expected of an attorney. It was why he had chosen to be an Estate Planning attorney rather than one that litigated for innocence or guilt. But that decision didn't change the fact that he was often told things he wished he didn't know, and he was sometimes angry with himself for taking a client that brought him those things to deal with.

As if I could know in advance, he said to himself. How could he know until they started talking?

Paul Mann had turned out to be one of those clients. But he didn't know that was going to be the case.

At first, Bruce thought that Paul's estate would be easy to plan. There was only his wife, and everything would go to her. But then, Paul added a twist.

When Bruce realized Paul wanted to tell him something he would rather not know and didn't affect the estate plan, Bruce had asked Paul to write it down instead and seal it in an envelope. Bruce would give it to Paul's wife when it was the right time.

And yes, he'd mail the letters after Paul's death. He understood Paul knew he was dying and had some things he wanted his wife to know.

"Why don't you just tell her now?" Bruce had asked.

"I can't. I don't want to see Bree's love for me die out before I die."

"And you think that might happen?"

"I can't take the chance. From the moment I first saw her, I knew I wanted to spend the rest of my life with her. I can't take that away from myself this last year together."

When Paul told him that story, Bruce had silently laughed to himself. Love at first sight was a myth projected through the media. How anyone could fall for that nonsense was beyond him.

But just a few minutes ago, when that woman Judith popped up on his screen, something happened. He had barely answered her questions, trying to keep himself in the place he always was when he spoke to people—especially clients.

But looking at her was like looking at a fire, and it started melting away his words and his thoughts.

She had stared at him, said, "Oh," and put her head down as if she was collecting her thoughts. Then she looked up and started asking questions. Questions he couldn't answer, even if he hadn't lost his mind at the sight of her.

Now, as Bruce breathed in the spring smell, trying to clear his mind, he asked the tree and the bees, "What do I do about this?"

He could have sworn that the tree shook a little, as if it was laughing, but perhaps it was only a gust of wind.

Twenty-Five

"Shall we stop for the night?" Cindy asked two hours later. They could make it to Pittsfield if they kept on driving, but it would be late, and they'd be tired. "The secret, whatever it is, will keep until tomorrow, at least."

"Sure, do you care where?"

Cindy's first thought was that anywhere would do, but would it? Wasn't Paul's intention, in part, to give Bree a last gift? Why not make it as pleasant as possible?

Before Cindy could answer, Bree started bouncing in her seat, looking at her phone.

"What?" Cindy asked.

"We're coming up on Corning, NY. I've always wanted to see the Corning Glass museum!"

Astonished, Cindy glanced over at Bree, who looked happy for the first time since she had come to get her.

Whatever Bree wants, Bree gets, Cindy said to herself, and out loud asked, "What exit?"

Bree used her phone, and within the hour, they checked into a Hilton hotel within walking distance to the museum. But by that time, it was almost four in the afternoon, and they decided to wait until morning to see the museum so they could fully enjoy it. After that, they'd head to Pittsfield.

Cindy texted Judith about their plans and asked her how things were going on at her end. Judith's answer of "just peachy-keen" made her laugh. That was Judith's favorite way of responding when things were not going according to how she thought things should go.

"What's up?" she texted back.

"Ah, nothing to worry about. Everything is fine."

Cindy knew enough not to argue with Judith. If Judith said it was fine, she meant she could handle it. Mostly she did. But not always, so she texted back: "I'm here if you need me."

Judith's response of a heart Emoji meant she was done talking about it, at least for now, so Cindy turned her attention to Bree, who was sitting cross-legged on the bed concentrating on her phone.

"What are you doing?"

"Making notes about this trip. It's a habit, I guess. Everything gives me ideas to write about, and I keep track of them just in case I need them later."

Bree put the phone down and leaned back on the stack of pillows behind her. She had taken a shower, and left her hair to dry on its own, so she had put a towel on the pillows to keep them dry.

Cindy could smell a faint hint of the flowery shampoo that Bree had used. She doubted it was one Bree usually used. Bree was more of a no scent kind of woman, but maybe that was then, and she was different now.

Well, of course, she's different now, Cindy thought. *Who isn't?* Except Cindy knew that Bree's difference didn't necessarily extend to the fact that time had passed, but more to what she had buried in the past.

"For the first time since Paul died, I have ideas and don't feel as if I am at the edge of a pool of quicksand and every memory will suck me under. I still feel like I am living inside a shell, but at least there is a stream of light coming through. That's thanks to you, Cindy. And the pact."

"We're here for you, as always."

Cindy didn't let herself think about how hurt she and the others had been at Bree's disappearance. Angry and hurt. But this wasn't the time to talk about that. Perhaps there never would be a time. Maybe it would fade away, or wonderful memories would override the bad ones.

Bree turned her phone towards Cindy. "Look what this says."

Cindy squinted. The beds were feet apart. There was no way she could see what was on the phone. She gave Bree a look, and Bree laughed.

"Sorry. This is the website of the Corning Museum of Glass. Its tag line is 'See glass in a new light.' It feels like a message to me. But instead of glass, it's my life. 'See my life in a new light.'

"The problem is, I know every piece of glass we see tomorrow will be beautiful. And I know that every piece of my life is not. And those are the parts that I know about. They are dark enough. But Paul had a secret, and it can't possibly be a good thing. Otherwise, he would have told me about it. It's got to be bad, doesn't it?"

Cindy sighed. "It seems that way. But I like your idea of seeing in a new light. Perhaps if we are not afraid of what we find, we'll see the opportunity.

"Not saying that it will be a good thing we discover, but it will release you from something that you didn't even know was holding you down. That's got to be a good thing, doesn't it?"

"Sure," Bree said, turning her phone face down on the table beside both their beds. She reached up and flipped out her light.

Cindy did the same, thinking they were both exhausted and sleep would come easy.

But then Bree giggled. "Remember when we were at a sleepover at April's house, and we hid everyone's clothes so they couldn't find them the next morning?"

Cindy laughed, "And then Judith lectured us about how it wasn't funny?"

For the next few hours, the two friends talked into the night just as they used to back in high school. The difference was that then they shared almost everything, and this time both of them knew they were avoiding the subject of Bree and Paul for the past thirty years.

Just before finally falling asleep, Bree said, "This secret that Paul kept from me feels like someone is in my house, robbing me. Someone who has been there all along, and I didn't know it. But I did. I just pretended he wasn't there."

"What counts is you are confronting it now, Bree."

"But, I am afraid," Bree whispered.

"Remember the light," Cindy whispered back.

Twenty-Six

"Well, for Pete's sake," Marsha shouted at the steering wheel of her car, slapping it at the same time. A woman getting into the car next to her gave her a look. Marsha shrugged, and the woman laughed.

Who hasn't yelled in their car at one time or another, Marsha thought.

Judith had just texted her that Cindy and Bree were stopping in Corning for the night and wouldn't be in Pittsfield until the following afternoon. Marsha had planned out her day carefully, knowing she was just over an hour away from Pittsfield.

Besides seeing the Taconic Sculpture Park, she had also visited the Ichabod Crane house and had a delightful lunch between visiting both places, basically basking in the beauty of the surroundings.

She planned to find out where the girls were having dinner and then pop in and surprise them. She had been playing it over in her head for the entire day, alternating between worry about how she would react and excitement over how they would respond.

After multiple imaginings, she realized that any resentment she felt would be overcome when she saw her friends again.

But now, that resentment was back. She had how it was going to happen all planned out. What was she supposed to do now? Marsha thought about turning around and going home. She'd had her fun. She'd cancel the sale of her home. Maybe even start up the school again. She was right. She couldn't count on anyone.

For Pete's sake, Marsha said again, this time just to herself. *Get over it! What are you, twelve?*

It was Bree's voice in her head that said those words to Marsha. Back when they were in high school, and things didn't go their way, that's what Bree would say to her when she would feel like running.

No more running, Marsha reminded herself.

She could go to Pittsfield as she planned and see what she could learn about why Paul Stanford Mann said it all began there—assuming that they were heading to the right place. Big assumption, but what else did they have?

A few hours later, she was checked into a hotel and had dinner and a long bath. Afterward, she rented a movie, watching it propped up in bed, surrounded by pillows and snacks. In the morning, she would check out the town. Maybe she'd have the complete mystery figured out before Bree and Cindy even got there.

A wave of jealousy came over her. She was alone while Bree and Cindy were together. But then, isn't that what she had chosen for herself? Besides, she would be back with them by tomorrow night. She'd be starting a new life.

No more running away, Marsha said to herself again. And if she had anything to say about it, none of them would run away anymore.

But, Marsha also knew that even though she had said she wasn't running, she had a secret. But it was one she might never, ever, share, and that was a form of running.

Although the hotel offered a breakfast of sorts, it wasn't enough for Marsha. Besides, everyone in the hotel was a stranger to Pittsfield. Marsha wanted to learn more about the people and start tracking down information about Paul. She already knew that the Internet was a bust.

Judith had told her how little there was out there about him, and if Judith looked, that was that. Judith would have hired people if she couldn't find any information on her own, so Marsha knew she would waste time if she looked for herself. That there was nothing had always seemed suspicious. Why so little information about Paul?

Marsha knew it was easier to disappear before social media and the documentation online of everyone's life, but why did they? After all, Paul had been the hunky professor, and Bree was always in charge of everything they did. Why did they walk away from that?

As Marsha ate breakfast with enough food that she would have previously spread out over three days, she pondered how they had all gotten to this place. Here she was in a strange town waiting for two women she had known her entire life, had made a pact with in second grade, but mainly ignored for the last thirty years. What had happened to them?

They had even named themselves. It was Cindy who had proposed it, of course.

Cindy and Bree were the first two members of the Ruby Sisters, having met in first grade. When they added new members, they held a little ceremony and were given a ruby. It was really a red glass bubble, but Cindy would always say that someday they would all have real ones.

"Why rubies?" Judith had asked, and Cindy explained she had learned that rubies were a symbol for both love and courage, and she figured they would need both in their life.

Besides, it reminded her of Dorothy's ruby slippers in the Wizard of Oz, and when they were together, they were home.

Well, it was true then, Marsha thought to herself. *We were family then, and we believed in love and courage. But we didn't stay together, and I'm not sure if I have had love and courage.*

No, she was sure. She had had little love and courage in her life since leaving Spring Falls. But returning to the Ruby Sisters and their pact was the first step into a new life.

Pouring another dollop of maple syrup onto the last of her pancakes and inhaling the smell of real maple syrup, Marsha suppressed the urge to burp and smiled to herself. She might not let herself eat like this again for a long time, but she didn't think she'd be performing on stage, or anywhere for that matter, so it didn't matter all that much.

When the waitress came to the table to give her the bill, Marsha asked where she could find old records about people who had lived in Pittsfield before.

"Before when, hon?" the waitress answered.

Thinking about Paul's age and when they all had first met him, she answered, "Between 1960 and 1989?"

"Well, I've lived here much of that time. Are you looking for something or someone in particular?"

"A man named Paul Stanford Mann?"

"Doesn't ring a bell. Lots of Pauls around, you know. And Mann? Nope, can't think that I knew anyone by that name."

"So if I were going to find him, where would I look?"

"Try the Berkshire Athenaeum. It's not far from here."

Seeing Marsha's puzzled look, she laughed and added, "It's our library, hon. You can walk from here if you want to."

Twenty-Seven

It had been an hour since she had talked to Judith, and now that she didn't have Judith encouraging her, April knew her intention to go to Spring Falls was fading.

What was she thinking? She was running away from the man that she loved. The man she had been married to for over thirty years. The father of her children. How could she be doing this, and why?

She knew Ron didn't realize she was gone yet, or he'd be calling and texting. And so far, the phone had been quiet. He had gone to work and ignored her and what he had done. April thought maybe she should call him and find out how he was feeling?

Besides, she had to use the restroom and get something to drink. She'd call Ron from there.

As she pulled into the gas station's parking lot, her phone rang. Thinking it might be Ron, her heart started beating faster. What would he say? Would he apologize? Would he explain why he was ready to hit her and didn't want her to go to her friends for a visit?

Instead, it was Judith. *Of course, it would be,* April thought, *She is checking up on me, just as she has all these years.* Reluctantly, she answered the phone.

"Where are you now?" Judith asked.

"About two hours away."

"What's going on? What are you thinking?"

When April didn't answer, Judith's commanding voice took over, and April felt her body shudder and then relax. She closed her eyes and listened.

"You can't go back right now, April. I know it's hard. But you aren't leaving him. You are simply coming to visit friends and help a friend who needs you."

April sighed but still said nothing.

"Has he called you?" Judith asked.

"No," she whispered.

"Does he usually call you during the day?"

For some reason, that question stunned April. No, he didn't call during the day. He never did. He left in the morning and came back at night—except when he didn't.

Sometimes he would be gone for work for days, never checking in with her. But he always returned so upbeat and happy to see her, after the first few times it happened, she had stopped questioning why she hadn't heard from him.

His attention to her and the kids when he was home made up for it. Or was that what she had been telling herself? The questions she was asking herself made her sick to her stomach.

When April didn't answer, Judith added, "I want you to do something for me. I don't know why I didn't think of it before. I'm going to ask Cindy, Bree, and Marsha to do the same thing."

"What?"

"I want us all to put the find-a-friend app on our phones. That way, we will know where all the Ruby Sisters are, and although we aren't in one place, we will still be together, just as we intended when we made our pact."

At first, April didn't like the idea, and then she thought about knowing where everyone was, and it brought her a sense of peace she hadn't experienced for a long time.

When they were young, they kept track of each other. They watched each other's moods, figured out if something bad was going on at home, and then came up with ways to distract and comfort.

Imagine what that would feel like to be in that space again. Besides, this way, even when I am at home, I'll still be part of the group, April said to herself.

"You're right. I was thinking of calling Ron and going home again," April admitted. "And I know that's not a good idea. He should call me, shouldn't he?"

April asked, knowing the answer already, and Judith knew she didn't have to reply to the question.

"Come and help me find out what Paul wanted us to know. I need help to figure this out, April. Cindy, Bree, and Marsha are looking in the town they think he came from, but I could use a friend and some help here.

"Besides, Cindy left her art gallery in my hands, and I keep checking in with the two women running it for her. Maybe you could do that for her and me until she returns."

A bolt of excitement ran through April, and she realized how different that felt from the bolt of fear she had felt a few hours earlier. And how different it felt, even if only for a moment, than the low-level anxiety and boredom she felt all the time—and hadn't noticed until now.

It made her wonder what else she hadn't noticed. Now was as good a time as ever to make a change, and watching over Cindy's art gallery was a great place to start.

"You're right," April said, not hearing but feeling Judith's sigh of relief.

Thirty minutes later, she had visited the restroom, got some snacks, and installed the app on her phone. So far, the only person on it was Judith, but knowing that Judith would talk to the other three that day, and soon all five of them would be a team again, gave her the same feeling of safety she had when they were growing up together and hadn't realized she had missed until now.

This time she set her GPS to Judith's home address in Spring Falls, knowing that would ensure that she wouldn't change her mind. Because April knew Judith would watch for her and make another call and get her to turn around if she did. She wouldn't put it past Judith to get in her car and come after her.

Judith had reminded her they were the "Z twins" after all. Even though April had taken Ron's last name, leaving her name of Zane behind, they were still the two who found each other in the back of the line in second grade.

April had laughed and agreed, but she knew that there was a reason other than wanting them all to be together that made Judith adamant about her leaving Ron, at least for now, and coming to Spring Falls.

It's only for a few weeks. It's not for good, April told herself. She'd wait until she got to Judith's before calling Ron at work. Or maybe she wouldn't call him at all and wait to see what he said when he discovered she wasn't at home.

Before pulling out of the parking lot, she tuned the radio to a station that played her favorite 1980s music. Ron didn't like the radio on when he was in the car, so it was a small act of rebellion. Going to Spring Falls was another.

The Traveling Wilburys' "End Of The Line" came on the radio. April laughed and started singing along while the lovely sounding

British voice on her GPS told her where to turn and how long it would take to get there.

Yes, I am doing things differently from now on, she said to herself. Inside, she acknowledged she was terrified. Despite that, it was time to find out what her life had been about and what she wanted from it now. She hoped it didn't mean she'd be without Ron. She loved him, but she needed some answers. Something was wrong. What wasn't he telling her?

Twenty-Eight

M arsha left her car in the restaurant's parking lot and did just what the waitress suggested. She walked to the library. It was a beautiful spring day, but she barely noticed.

By the time she got to the library, she had hashed over in her mind multiple scenarios about what she would find, or not find. In her imagination, she walked in, asked the librarian for the perfect place to look for someone who may or may not have lived in Pittsfield, and found Paul and his story within an hour.

By the time she had reached the library, Marsha had almost convinced herself that it was true.

It was only when she tried to explain what she was looking for that she realized how impossible this task would be. The librarian smiled and said they had several resources that she could look through to see if she could find the man she was looking for.

"Have you looked online?" was the librarian's first question after first introducing herself as Kathy. Marsha told Kathy her name and then answered that she hadn't, but her friend had, and there was nothing.

Kathy paused and then asked, "Have you thought that perhaps he wasn't using the name you knew him by?"

Marsha rocked back on her heels as all her hopes of finding Paul vanished. It was a complete waste of time. But because it was Paul who had sent them on this trip and they had to find out why, she asked the next question, when what she really wanted to do was go back to the hotel and maybe even back to bed.

"Well, if that was true, how can I ever find him?"

"How important is this?" Kathy asked.

"Very," Marsha answered, and then gave Kathy a brief scenario of why they were looking.

After hearing the story, Kathy said, "It's essential then, so let's assume he knew you'd come here, and look for what he meant by the statement, 'this is where it started.'

"If, as you say, he kept this secret for a long time and only after his death was willing for his wife to find out about it, then it might have been something that happened that got written up in the newspaper.

"You could go through old newspapers looking for a story that might have caused someone to run away and maybe even change their name."

Marsha now envisioned herself locked into an endless and perhaps fruitless search instead of getting an immediate answer. She would need the help of Cindy and Bree to do this, but at least she could get started.

Kathy and Marsha talked about possible scenarios and decided that Paul must have been at least a teenager when whatever happened, happened.

And because Paul had been teaching at Spring Falls Community College for two years before Bree had claimed him for her husband, they could narrow the timeframe. Having reduced the search down to only fifteen years, Marsha settled in front of the microfiche machine and began the search.

"Let me know if you need more," Kathy said. "I have a few other ideas about places where you can look."

Marsha nodded and began the task of reading old newspapers, searching for any story that might have triggered someone to hide from it for their entire life. Within a few hours, she was both depressed and frustrated.

Focusing on bad news, she had found so much of it she had to keep reminding herself that life was good because there were enough fires, accidents, murders, abductions, and other assorted tragedies it could destroy anyone's belief in the quality of God's grace.

Even though Marsha never thought of herself as a religious person, she kept herself sane most of the time by believing that grace existed and she could find it if she looked for it hard enough.

But after four hours of searching through tragedies, she questioned if that was true. Where was a god in all of that?

Time to get out of here, she told herself.

She was depressed and uncomfortable. Her hair was sticking to the back of her neck—she hated hair on her neck. She either needed to keep it up in the dancer's bun or get it cut.

Plus, the waistband of her pants was digging into her sides. *Either stop eating so much or go to elastic waistbands*, she told herself. It would probably be elastic waistbands because she was hungry again.

Besides, she needed to get ready to surprise Cindy and Bree. She had written a list of likely events that might have been Paul's trigger for running away.

Of course, there was no boy, or young man, named Paul in any of the stories. That would have been too easy. But Marsha had decided that it was possible—probable—that he had changed his name.

Marsha stopped by the front desk on her way out of the library and thanked Kathy for her help.

"Did you find anything?"

Gesturing to the notes in her hand, Marsha answered, "Yes. Lots of terrible things that happened, but nothing specific for the man I'm looking for."

"Well, when I get depressed over all the bad stuff in the world, I remind myself of two things."

"What are they?"

"That they are far outweighed by the good things that I take for granted, and to look for God's grace in the helpers, as Mr. Rogers said."

Tears popped up in Marsha's eyes, surprising her. "Thank you for the reminder. I'll be back tomorrow with a few friends to look again."

"I'll be here, and I have some ideas of other places to look. Didn't you say that this man meant this search and what you find to be a gift to his widow?"

Marsha nodded, brushing away a tear that had escaped. "But I'm afraid we are going to find some terrible things that will be painful for her."

Kathy came around from the back of the desk where she had been standing and reached out to hold both of Marsha's hands.

"But the secret has been painful all along, don't you think? Yes, you and your friends might have to face some terrible truths, but then the healing can begin."

Marsha and Kathy exchanged a brief hug as Marsha whispered, "Thank you."

As Kathy watched Marsha walk away, she reached into her desk drawer, pulled out a letter, and then made a phone call to the number listed there. She had not understood the letter when she first received it and had almost forgotten about it, thinking it might be a prank.

But when she heard Marsha's story that morning, she remembered it and wondered if this woman was the one the letter mentioned would show up one day. At first, she hadn't thought so but then realized that Marsha wasn't the woman the letter referred to, but that woman would be in town soon.

As Kathy made the phone call, she wondered who the lawyer would be contacting. All she knew was that someone would come to help the searchers, and she got to be part of the solution.

God's grace," she said to herself. *Look for it in the helpers.*

Twenty-Nine

Marsha made it back to her car in a daze, no longer hopeful that they would find Paul. Yes, they would go back to the library and look again in the morning, but she was reasonably sure it was a lost cause.

Marsha could feel the all too familiar self-pity and discouragement trying to take over, but she kept pushing it away using the mantras that usually worked. She had no time for her mood swings. She had to get ready for the Bree and Cindy surprise.

Settling into the front seat of the car and opening all the windows to let in some fresh air, Marsha checked the find-a-friends app that Judith had asked her to install. She did it because Judith asked her to, but now, looking at it and seeing all four of the Ruby Sisters' names and their location moved her from self-pity to gratitude. They were together again. How had she let that part of her life slip away?

She could see April had arrived in Spring Falls. Judith had told her that April was coming to help them. But the catch in Judith's voice made her think there was more to the story than that, because, as far as she knew, this was the first time April had visited without Ron. She wasn't even sure they had ever come back after Paul and Bree's wedding.

Part of Marsha hoped that meant Ron would stay away, but then berated herself. April loved him. She needed to accept that he was also part of their group, just as Paul was.

The realization that there were no other men took her by surprise. Why not? Out of the five Ruby Sisters, only two of them had relationships? Perhaps it was something they could explore together. But not now, maybe never. She knew why there wasn't a man for her, but that was not something she would ever share, even with her friends, especially with these friends.

Marsha made sure she allowed all of them to find her on their find-a-friend app and then realized that meant that Bree and Cindy would know she was in Pittsfield.

Well, that surprise is ruined, Marsha thought, *unless they don't look at the app.*

At that moment, her phone rang, and Cindy was shouting and sobbing.

"You're there? How did that happen? Where are you? Why are you?"

Marsha answered the last question, since all the answers to the other questions were obvious.

"I wanted to surprise you."

"Well, it worked! We can't believe it. Bree is driving, so she can't talk, but where can we meet?"

"Why not register in the same hotel as me? I'll meet you in the lobby."

Thirty minutes later, three women ran towards each other screaming and crying, causing everyone near to turn in alarm.

But when it was apparent that it was a joyous reunion, they smiled before turning away, feeling better about the world, if only for a moment.

Thirty

The three friends chose room service. They remembered being asked to leave restaurants in their youth because their laughing and giggling bothered people, and being older would not stop them from doing the same thing. Besides, this time, they knew there would be some sobbing as well.

They ordered what they used to order. Two pizzas, both loaded with everything, except half of one was meatless for Bree, as it had been since high school.

"Doesn't it feel as if we have never been apart?" Cindy asked, looking at two friends she had known almost her entire life.

They had pulled a table between the two beds and put the pizzas, sodas, and stacks of napkins on it. Marsha sat on one bed, her legs crossed, and Cindy and Bree sat on the edge of the other bed.

Tipping her head back to get the long string of cheese hanging off her pizza into her mouth, Marsha mumbled, "Yes and no."

All three fell silent, thinking how long it had been since they had been together.

It was Bree who broke the silence. "I'm sorry."

She didn't need to explain what she was sorry for, but there was a long silence before Marsha asked, "Why did you leave and then stay away, Bree?"

Bree shook her head. "I can't tell you. I'm sorry I can't, I just can't."

Cindy put her arm around her friend, and Bree let herself lean in for a moment.

"Well, it doesn't matter now, does it? We're together again, and besides, we have a mystery to solve."

Marsha watched as panic flashed in Bree's hazel eyes and wondered if this was a mystery that Bree was afraid to solve. It was understandable. It had to be hard to worry if your husband was who you thought he was and what secret he had kept all these years.

Maybe she doesn't want to know, Marsha thought. *Perhaps she is still running from the truth. Bree could be lying about what Paul said. She's the one who led us here. Maybe we are on a wild goose chase.*

But Marsha knew Bree well. It would go against everything Bree believed in to lie to them. Bree had never lied to them before. Yes, she ran away, but probably to keep from lying about something.

Marsha understood that. Hadn't she done the same thing? Maybe she hadn't disappeared the way Bree and Paul did, but she had kept away to keep her own secret.

As if she knew what Marsha was thinking, Bree said, "I do want to understand why Paul wrote those letters. He wanted me to know something. Something he was afraid to tell me when he was alive.

"And yes, I am terrified to find out what it is. Was Paul the man I thought I married? Was the life we lived a lie? It didn't feel like one. But what if I am wrong, and he wasn't who I thought he was?"

"And what if he was?" Cindy said. "What if he kept from you whatever this secret is because he was afraid to tell you, afraid of how you would feel about it? But if it happened before you met him, then I think he should have trusted you with it."

Marsha nodded. "Yes, perhaps he should have, but Bree, you know how it is. Telling someone something you have kept secret for a long time can make it into a bigger thing than it is. Maybe that's what happened with Paul."

Bree gave Marsha a long look, and for a moment, Marsha was afraid that she had revealed something she hadn't meant to reveal. But then Bree looked away, and Cindy said, "And now he wants you to know. He could have left it alone, and he didn't. Perhaps that means it's going to be a good thing for you.

"And if nothing else, he has given us a gift of getting us all together. April is with Judith in Spring Falls, and we'll see them when we find what we need to find here."

Bree patted Cindy on the hand as she smiled at Marsha and said, "That will be wonderful, won't it?" before standing and heading to the bathroom.

When she was gone, Cindy whispered to Marsha, "She doesn't seem thrilled about going to Spring Falls, does she? Doesn't she want to see Judith and April?"

"Maybe what she ran away from is still there?"

"Probably. Or at least Bree is afraid that it is. Is what you ran from still there, Marsha?"

"I didn't run away. I ran towards. You know why. I wanted to be a Broadway sensation, singing and dancing on stage forever. New York was fun and exciting, but I wasn't as good as I thought I was. However, even though I was never the sensation I had hoped to be, I did do some small things."

"Did you love it as much as you expected?"

"More. I loved it more than I expected. But the parts I could play became fewer and fewer, and I gave up. Moved away and started a small dance school. Made a living."

"A living, but not a life?"

Marsha uncrossed her legs and started clearing the table. Cindy joined her, neither one of them speaking. When they finished, Marsha looked down at her friend. People always teased them when they were together.

Tall Marsha. almost as tall as Judith, and short Cindy. She wondered if it had bothered Cindy to be teased about being so small. Cindy and April were the short ones in the group, although April was the smallest. Did they mind?

She had never asked. Maybe that was why she hadn't had a life. She had never asked others how they felt. Yes, she thought about how they felt, but never asked.

Perhaps that was why Cindy was right about her. She had made a living, but not a life. She was more worried about her feelings, worried that people didn't care enough to be there for her when she needed them. So she set herself apart so they wouldn't let her down. She let them down instead.

Marsha looked at Cindy, her blue eyes still clear and kind, wanting, as always, to be helpful. Marsha sighed and looked away before answering.

"You're right, Cindy. It was a living, but not a life. But I want one now."

Bree had come out of the bathroom, heard what Marsha said, and reached out for both Cindy and Marsha's hands before saying, "Me too. I made a living. And I had a life with Paul, but it's gone, and it's possible that what I thought was real was all a lie. So, me, too, Marsha, I want to build a new life now."

"Well," Cindy said, laughing and breaking the somber mood, "The pact lives on!"

"And solves mysteries together," Marsha added.

"And solves mysteries together," Bree agreed.

And even though her head was pounding because of the fear she felt at what they would find, she didn't care. She'd been living in the dark too long.

Yes, it was time to build a new life for herself, and this time she would do it with her friends.

Thirty-One

Ron came home at the same time as he always came home. He knew how important it was for April to have a feeling of security, and keeping a schedule that made her life with him safe and comfortable was easy to do.

When he had to go out of town, April understood he couldn't check-in, but he always returned to her, and April accepted that as enough.

Besides, she had told him it gave her a sense of freedom to do her own thing while he was gone. Neither of them added that her freedom remained within previously set guidelines. But that was only to keep her safe.

Ron thought back to the first time he saw April in class. She was perfect. Her brown curly hair made a kind of halo around her head when the light hit it a certain way, and when April turned her dark brown eyes to him, he felt as if he was the most important person in the world to her. She had captivated him from the beginning. She was his rock—always there for him and the kids.

It was uncharacteristic of him to have lost his temper that morning. He was proud of how cool and logical he always was, so it took him by surprise almost as much as it surprised April. And his anger and frustration had built until he was afraid of it himself and had to leave before he did something he regretted.

But it had been a one-time thing, and he was sure April would have forgotten it by now. They had an agreement. They were a unit together. When they were in college, they even named themselves Unit One. Their favorite song was "Just The Two Of Us."

April gave him the freedom to be himself, and she was always there for him, as he was for her. Their children were an extension of the two of them. But now that the children had moved away, and they were back to just the two of them, he was even happier than before.

Then she got that letter and started talking about visiting Spring Falls, and to him, that meant she was breaking their agreement.

He was so used to her wanting and needing just him it had shocked him that she would think of needing anyone or anything else.

That's what had set him off. April said she was going even if he wasn't happy about it. Hadn't just the two of them always been enough? Wasn't it enough that she and Judith talked almost every week?

Yes, he knew about that. He hadn't liked it, but it seemed harmless enough until that morning when he realized it was a crack in his control that he should have shut down long ago.

Didn't April know he only wanted to keep their life the way it always had been? And of course, that's what she wanted too. She just had forgotten for a moment.

So sure was Ron that he and April were still and always Unit One, that when he opened the garage door and didn't see her car, he wasn't worried. She had probably dashed off to the store to get something she needed for their dinner.

Only when he smelled nothing cooking, and the mess was still on the floor underneath a towel, did he feel the tremor of anxiety and anger. April knew what time he would be home and what time he expected dinner. It was always waiting for him. And if she ran off to the store, there would be something cooking and a note.

But there was neither. No note. Nothing in the oven. A dirty floor. Completely unlike his wife. The house felt cold. April hated the cold and kept the heat on, even in the spring. Where was she?

A frisson of fear spread throughout his body, temporarily overriding the anger. What if something happened to April?

He knew bad things happened to people. What if they happened to his April? Moving quickly through the dining room and living room, he saw no signs of disturbance.

Maybe she's upstairs sleeping, he said to himself, forgetting that her car wasn't in the garage.

But she wasn't. And it was only then that Ron let himself see what was obvious. April wasn't home, even though she expected him to be.

"No," he shouted to the empty bedroom. April had to be there! She was the light of his life, the rock that held their life together.

Collapsing on the bed, he dropped his head into his hands and moaned. What had he done? He couldn't lose her. He had made a mistake. It had seemed so minor to him, but he had been wrong. It hadn't been minor to April.

Had he broken their life forever? It couldn't be. He wouldn't let that happen.

Trying her phone, it just rang and rang. He hung up before her message came on. What could he say? Apologize? What would she want to hear that would bring her back and restore their unit?

Opening the closet, he saw that some of her clothes were missing, and so was his suitcase. Now he was terrified. She had his suitcase.

151

He wanted to tear into everything in the bedroom and wreck it. But he knew that would not help. It wouldn't bring April back to him.

No, he needed to do what she wanted. She wanted him to be with her where she felt she needed to go. He should have understood. If he hadn't been so satisfied with their lives, he might have noticed the crack in her satisfaction. And he could have fixed it.

But it wasn't too late. He would go to Spring Falls and be there for her. Then, once she had that out of her system, they could come home and return to the life he loved.

No, he didn't want to go back to Spring Falls, but it had been years since they had been there. Perhaps all the reasons he didn't want to return were gone.

And even if they weren't, April was the most essential thing in the world to him. Nothing had changed that for him. He thought about texting April and telling her he was coming to see her, and then decided that it would be better to surprise her.

Besides, he needed some food and a good night's sleep before going. And he needed a new suitcase. He would stay with her in Spring Falls until she was ready to come home. As long as it took, he had patience. April still loved him. He was sure of that.

Besides, there was this mystery about why Paul and Bree had left, and the girls were off chasing it. It might be fun to be part of that unraveling. Perfect Paul might not be so perfect after all.

If there was one thing Ron was sure of it was that no one was as perfect as they seemed to be. Well, almost no one. April was, and he would do whatever it took to get her back. In the morning.

He was sure she'd be waiting for him. Maybe waiting for him would help her see the mistake she had made. If not, he'd do the waiting until she did.

Thirty-Two

"What if we throw you a belated birthday party?" Judith asked April, putting her favorite sandwich in front of her.

Judith was trying everything she could to cheer April up, but it wasn't Judith's strong suit, and she was failing. April had arrived distraught and stressed, and Judith hoped the sandwich and birthday party idea might make her feel better.

April attempted to smile, but it felt more like a grimace. She thanked Judith for remembering how much she liked peanut butter sandwiches with raspberry preserves, sliced bananas, and a few potato chips on top of the bananas.

She knew that Judith probably didn't have any of these ingredients and had shopped for them just for her and she sincerely appreciated the effort. Still, April felt as if a hundred-pound weight was pinning her underwater, and she had to keep struggling to breathe. She ate half the sandwich and then said she was too tired to eat more.

Judith wrapped the other half of the sandwich. She put it in the refrigerator just in case April got hungry in the night and then took her upstairs to the guest bedroom and tucked her in, leaving a night light on since she knew April didn't like to sleep in totally dark rooms.

Judith did all of this from the place inside of her that took care of things, keeping at bay the part of her that wanted to grab Ron around the neck and shake him.

There are two sides to every story, she kept saying to herself, but seeing her friend in such distress made what the Ruby Sisters called "the warrior queen" come alive. Righting wrongs was her thing.

Sometimes it was just numbers that added up wrong or ideas that someone didn't think through correctly, but when people did something for the wrong reasons, it made her furious, and she wanted to challenge them and make it right no matter what it took.

Her warrior queen quality made her great at her job but sometimes terrible at friendships, which is why she treasured her friendship with the Ruby Sisters. Throughout school, no matter what, they stuck together and loved her even when she embarrassed them or called them out. And she was grateful it worked both ways. They weren't afraid to tell her when she was wrong, too. Back then, they had always worked it out together. She hoped it would be like that again.

Sitting in the dark at her desk after putting April to bed, she had to ask herself if it was true that they had stuck together. Because if they had, would April be in such a mess, or Bree, Cindy, and Marsha looking for past mysteries? And maybe that was why she was so angry? Perhaps she was mad at herself for not finding Bree and Paul, for not going to see Marsha when she moved away.

Yes, she had kept in touch with April, but had she? How had she not noticed that April never came to visit? She had visited April and Ron in Silver Lake after their first child was born. But it was so obvious that April and Ron liked to be alone that she felt like an intruder.

Besides, her work only allowed her to leave for a day or two at a time. She ran a tight ship, and that took constant supervision. The independent accountants and bookkeepers that she hired appreciated her clarity and exactness. They always knew what she wanted and needed, and in return, she took great care of them.

But they weren't her friends. She had only four friends, and she had let at least three of them down by not being more diligent. Perhaps she had even let Cindy down and didn't notice it. She'd deal with that later.

The following day, looking at April sitting on the couch looking miserable, she tried again. "Okay, not a birthday party right now. Maybe when everyone gets here? We could have a party for all our birthdays and all the ones we missed together these past thirty years."

April smiled at Judith, thinking how the years had not softened her spirit and how much she appreciated that Judith had opened her home to give her time to try to understand what had happened to her relationship with Ron.

Perhaps what happened was a one-time thing, and she should go home.

As if she heard her thoughts, Judith said, "Let's go out to breakfast, and then I'll take you over to Cindy's art gallery and show you how it works so you can help out. But we need to stop at the store on the way to pick up cat food."

"Cat food?"

"Yep. Cindy's gallery cat. Not an alley cat, gallery cat. Everyone laughs when she says that. Cindy swears people come in to see the cat and then notice the art."

It delighted Judith to see April's face light up. Maybe the cat was the way to April's heart. She remembered April talking about her hippy parents and the multitude of cats that came in and out of their house. And all the neighbors that had the same thing at their house. April had loved all the hustle and bustle of cats and people.

At the time, none of them had known how devastating outdoor cats were to their beloved bird population. Once April's parents and friends realized what was happening to the birds, they kept the cats indoors.

But the people kept coming. There was always something going on at April's childhood home. On one of their calls, April had confided to Judith that she had always wanted to get cats for her and the kids, but Ron had said he was allergic, so they hadn't.

For a moment, April wondered how her life had gotten so small when she had loved the crazy outgoing life of her childhood. Her parents were long gone, and maybe that's why she had let that life go, too. And now, she might be ready to get it back, starting with Cindy's gallery cat.

"What's its name?"

"Mittens," Judith answered. "Where do you want to go to breakfast?"

"Is the Waffle House still open?"

"Of course it is! Can you be ready in thirty minutes? I have a few emails to send before we go."

Thirty minutes later, April freshly showered, her wet hair springing into curls around her face, they headed out the door.

Judith pointed to April's hair. "Still letting it do its own thing?"

April paused for a moment before answering. "I am. I think it may be the only thing I let stay itself."

Judith reached down and hugged April and laughed. "Well, young lady, it's about time that stops!"

April nodded, feeling the weight of her decision, and at the same time, for the first time in a long time, feeling a little like the bird her parents used to call her.

"Our little wren," they would croon as they enveloped her in hugs. It had been years since she heard their voices in her head calling her that. Perhaps it had been too painful to remember.

But now that she was in Spring Falls, it was as if a door had opened into her past. Was she ready to face it all? she asked herself and realized she would have to be, because the future was already set in motion.

Thirty-Three

Marsha, Bree, and Cindy agreed to meet in the lobby at 8:00 in the morning. They would have breakfast and then head to the library, which opened at 9:00.

Marsha had slept like the dead and barely heard her alarm clock go off, so she had scrambled to get ready, pulling her hair up into a bun, thinking that eventually, she was going to cut it all off.

The three of them had stayed up long into the night talking books and movies and their favorite plants and all sorts of things they would have talked about over the years if they had been together.

What they didn't talk about was why they were there. It was a night of lovely memories and getting caught up on the trivia of life.

Judith had called after putting April to bed, and even though they were worried about April, all five of them felt safe for the moment. Not that anyone knew what they were safe from, but it felt that way, so they went with it because they knew that what happened—or didn't happen—at the library would be a pivot point in all their lives.

They would either find something, and that would change everything. Or they wouldn't. And then they would have to decide whether to continue looking or try to help Bree rebuild her life on secrets.

After Marsha had gone to her room, Bree turned out the light and wished sweet dreams to Cindy, who was already half asleep. Bree envied her. Since Paul had died, she had barely slept, running what-if scenarios around and around in her head.

Bree knew this was not a wise thing to be doing. As a child, she had learned how to shut down the creative part of her brain at night so she could sleep anytime, anywhere. Paul said she could sleep through anything, which was true when he was alive.

Since Paul's death, her superpower of sleeping everywhere had disappeared. Now she was a restless sleeper. First, because of the grief and the hollow place inside herself that missed Paul so much. It was a physical pain as if someone had chopped off her arms and legs.

Then the letter and the mystery and suspicions it brought with it kept her awake. She'd review their life together over and over, always wondering what about it had been true and what had been a lie.

That Paul had called his letter a last gift felt like the worst blow of all. How could he not know how painful it was to get that letter? What about searching for a secret he had kept from her all that time could be a gift?

At night, lying in the dark, staring at the ceiling searching for answers, Bree thought maybe he meant the road trip was the gift. Or perhaps it was the gift of bringing the Ruby Sisters back together. Is that what he meant? Did he think a road trip would be enough of a gift to override what they would find?

Besides, although the road trip got her out of the house, it wasn't truly a road trip if all it did was send her to one rest stop and one town.

Maybe all he wanted her to do was move out of her old life and into a new one. Perhaps he thought a change of scenery would give her a chance to think more clearly.

But it wasn't working. She wasn't thinking more clearly. There were more questions than answers. And the answers weren't something she was looking forward to discovering. All she wanted to do was finish the search and then try to move on.

So when their alarm rang at 7:00 a.m., Bree felt worse than she did before she went to bed. Cindy, on the other hand, rolled over and smiled at her, drowsy but looking well-rested.

"Woke up early?" Cindy asked, after shutting off the alarm.

"Didn't sleep well," Bree muttered, almost unwilling to admit that she was still a mess.

"I'm sorry," Cindy said as she shuffled to the bathroom and then shouted through the bathroom door, "But today we get answers!"

"Sure," Bree answered.

Can't wait, she said to herself and then wanted to slap herself for the resentment she had said it with.

Underneath all her sadness was a fury and resentment about everything and that made her want to scream in frustration. It wasn't fair to Cindy and Marsha, who only wanted to help.

By the time she and Cindy made it to the lobby where Marsha was waiting for them, Bree had managed to tamp her frustration down, but she knew it was still there, just waiting for a match to be thrown on it before it exploded and hurt everyone around her.

Marsha took them to the same place she had breakfast the day before, and the same waitress waited on them.

"Did you find the library okay, hon?" she asked before asking Marsha if she wanted the same breakfast.

"Yes, and no, just toast and coffee today," Marsha answered, still full from the pizza they had last night. Or else too anxious about the day.

"And you, hon?" she asked, looking at Bree and Cindy.

Bree just pointed to the short stack of pancakes, trying not to scream at the waitress that she wasn't her "hon."

Cindy asked for the same thing and inched herself away from Bree, afraid to touch her by mistake, feeling as if she was sitting beside a powder keg ready to explode.

After the waitress was gone, Cindy said, "It feels as if something is going to happen today."

"Is it good or bad?" Bree asked, hearing the resentment in her voice and hating herself for it once again.

"I guess that depends on how we view it," Cindy replied.

Bree wanted to smack Cindy. That ever-present optimist. How would she know how it felt to lose everything?

All that she was and all that she had with Paul was gone. Cindy had it easy. She always had. And yet Bree knew that wasn't true. She was taking out her fear on her best friend since first grade, and she hated herself even more for doing it.

"I'm sorry," Bree said, knowing that Cindy would understand that she was apologizing for feeling such an irrational anger towards the friends who were there for her.

"Nothing to be sorry about," Cindy answered, and Marsha nodded in agreement. "That was a flippant answer," Cindy added. "And I should know better. Whatever we find or don't find today, we'll be here for you, and if you want to yell and be mad, go ahead and be that. We understand."

Bree dropped her head, afraid to show her feelings, as always. And her friends, as always, carried on eating as if nothing had happened, letting her gather herself and be strong again. Even though she wasn't, they would let her pretend she was. Maybe someday she would be again.

Thirty-Four

After breakfast, they walked to the library, where Kathy greeted Marsha with a smile.

After introducing Bree and Cindy to Kathy, Marsha asked her if she had any new ideas about where to look for Paul's information.

"A few," Kathy said, and then, turning to Bree, reached out and held both her hands as she said, "I'm sorry for your loss."

Bree nodded and looked away as Kathy led them to a table where she had laid out yearbooks from local high schools. Bree knew if she were her usual self, she would enjoy the soft quiet safety of the library.

But at the moment, it felt ominous, as if it was filled with lost people crying out to her to be found, which was ridiculous. No one was lost, not even Paul. He was dead, not lost. All she wanted to do was run and hide from it all.

She recognized the feeling. She had run away with Paul. What bothered her most was Paul had run with her, knowing her secret. But she had never known his.

Did that mean that all of their life together was a lie? Bree wasn't sure she could live with that, and she didn't know if she had to either.

"Perhaps you will find him in one of these?"

"Thank you," Bree mumbled, looking at the stacks of books on the long table, smelling the mustiness of them. Did she really want to look through them? Wasn't this a waste of time?

But Cindy had already settled into a chair and patted one beside her.

"I'll look at the names, and you look at the faces," Cindy said, handing a yearbook to her.

Bree knew Cindy was implying that maybe Paul Stanford Mann wasn't his name at all, and that part was the beginning of the lies. Cindy was right. He might have changed his name. But would she recognize him?

Bree's frustration deepened. She could feel the fire inside her smoldering. It was a fruitless mission, but at least when they had no place else to look, she could call off the search knowing they had done their best, and perhaps that fire waiting to erupt could be put out for good.

Kathy touched Marsha's arm to get her attention and then tilted her head towards the rows of books that stood at the end of the room.

"I'll continue looking through old newspapers while you two look through these?" Marsha said, as she turned to follow Kathy.

"There's something I have to tell you," Kathy whispered as she led her back through a long row of books, checking to see that no one was around.

"What's going on?"

Kathy reached into her pocket, pulled out a folded-up piece of paper, and handed it to Marsha.

"I got this a few weeks ago. I thought it was a prank but held onto it because I didn't know what to make of it. And then yesterday, you walked into the library and asked to search for Paul Stanford Mann, and well... here, read it."

Marsha unfolded the paper and saw that it was a letter, just like the letters they had all received. Only Kathy's instructions were different.

Looking up from the letter, she asked, "You got a letter from Paul? How could that be? Did you know him?"

"No. Of course not, or I would have told you. The name sounded familiar when you asked about him, but I didn't associate it with the letter until after you left. I was worried all night. I hope I did the right thing. I followed the directions and called that lawyer and told him you were here."

Marsha felt like sitting on the floor and crying. It was a weird response, but that's what she wanted to do. Just sit down and cry. Make all of this go away. Go home wherever that was and start over somehow.

But seeing Kathy's distressed face, she pulled herself together and asked, "What did he say?"

"He said thanks and then hung up. Called me back ten minutes later and asked me if I could keep you here until some woman showed up."

"What woman? When is she coming?"

"I don't know who the woman is; he didn't tell me. The only thing he said was she would get here early this afternoon and would help your search for Paul. He only told me her name, and he said she would ask for me when she got here."

"Her name?"

"Grace. He said her name was Grace."

"What do I do?" Marsha asked Kathy as if she had the answers. "Do I tell them, or do we wait to see if this woman actually shows up?"

"Why not continue the search? That way, you might be better prepared for this Grace person and whatever she will tell you. At least it will keep you all here."

"For five more hours? I am not sure Bree will make it that long. I think she wants to forget the whole thing and leave as soon as possible."

"Can't blame her. Maybe search for a few hours and then go to lunch. I know a lovely restaurant close to here. When Grace arrives, I'll bring her there? In the meantime, I'll keep Cindy and Bree busy with yearbooks, and you keep checking the newspapers."

Marsha sighed before saying, "Okay."

She didn't have a better plan. Besides, who was this Grace? And what did she know that was so important she had to travel to Pittsfield to tell them? Was it someone Paul knew? Would she unravel the mystery for them? Would it be a good thing?

For a moment, Marsha thought about telling Cindy and Bree about the woman coming to meet them, but seeing Bree's pale face as she slowly looked through yearbooks, she decided against it. Bree was trying to be the strong woman they all knew, but it was evident that she was barely holding it together.

Marsha only hoped Grace was bringing good news, and Bree could begin to heal, but she doubted that was what it would be. Instead, it was much more likely to be something that tore Bree's life apart just a little bit more.

"Thanks, Paul," Marsha whispered sarcastically to his ghost. "Good thing you're not around right now because I am so angry with you I could punch you."

That thought made Marsha laugh. *Sure, I'd punch him. Not likely. Even so, he'd be feeling the wrath of four women, which is probably why he left.*

"Coward," she whispered again to him and headed back to the microfiche machine to see what she could find, but mostly to keep herself busy until Grace could get there.

It's funny how grace is precisely what we need right now, Marsha thought. *We need a moment or two of grace.*

Marsha wondered if the woman matched her name. She hoped that she did.

Thirty-Five

A s soon as they opened the back door to the gallery, a black cat with white paws streaked towards them and started rubbing herself against Judith's leg.

April reached down and picked up the cat, cooing at her as if she was a baby, and after a moment's hesitation, Mittens snuggled into her arms and purred. April felt as if her heart would burst and smiled at Judith with the smile Judith had not seen for years.

"I see why they call her Mittens," April said, holding up one of the four white paws. "And why people come to see her."

Apparently happy to meet a stranger, Mittens rubbed her face against April's and purred even louder.

Judith led the two of them into a tiny kitchen, and as soon as Mittens saw the bag of cat food, she was down on the floor, looking up expectantly with large green eyes. April's heart melted even more.

"May I stay all day with her?"

"Of course," Judith said. "Cindy's staff, Mimi and Janet, can use the help, and you could learn all about what Cindy is doing here. You might have some ideas to make it even better.

"The gallery opens in an hour. I'll show you around, introduce you to the staff, and then leave you here with Miss Mittens. I'll pick you up at the end of the day and take you to dinner. Or call me if you want to leave earlier than that."

April took a deep breath, looked around the tidy kitchen, walked out into the gallery, and spun in a circle. "No, I think I will be fine being here all day."

More than fine, she said to herself.

Here there was beauty and creativity. Outside the gallery windows, she could see the town that she had loved. She could explore the streets, learn about Cindy's art business, play with a cat, even sit in the coffee shop that now existed across the street and read a book.

The day was entirely hers to do with it what she wanted. There was no one expecting her to prepare a meal or clean the house or be home at a specific time. She'd meet strangers. She'd make new friends. The whole day stretched before her, filled with things that she had not realized she had missed.

Until that moment, it had not occurred to her that she spent most of her life pleasing her husband. It was time to find out what pleased her. The thought of it was both exhilarating and terrifying.

By the time Judith finished showing April around the gallery, the back door had opened, and two young women entered, smiling at Judith and at Mittens as she curled around both their legs in greeting.

Judith introduced April as an old friend to both her and Cindy and explained that April would help around the gallery until Cindy got back. Would Janet and Mimi show her the ropes?

"Ask me to do anything," April said. "I am eager to be helpful and learn as much as I can."

Both women smiled and shook her hand.

"We would love some help," the tall one named Mimi said.

"Are you an artist?" the shorter one named Janet asked.

April took a deep breath and then smiled. "I don't know. But I do know this feels like home to me."

"Well then, welcome home," Janet said, and Mimi nodded in agreement.

"On that note," Judith said, "I'll leave you three to your day. Call me if you need anything."

"Right, boss!" Janet said, mock saluting her. Judith laughed and said, "And don't you go forgetting it!"

"Don't worry," Janet said, seeing April's face. "Judith knows we love her. Cindy owns the gallery, of course, but everyone knows Judith makes sure it runs well. Actually, I think she makes sure the whole town runs well. I want to grow up to be just like her."

April smiled at the two of them and said, "I think I do too!"

Ron was not happy. After all, he had driven to this hated town, expecting to find April at Judith's, and instead found an empty house. With cameras. That meant that Judith knew he was there, and he didn't know where she was. He didn't like that dynamic at all.

Knowing that Judith would see his face on the camera, he waved to one and mouthed, "See you later," to it, hoping it appeared friendly and not ominous.

He needed to get over his anger at April for leaving and making him come back here. He used to love this town. Maybe he could at least like it again. And being angry at April would not get him what he wanted.

Driving away from Judith's, Ron knew he should call April and let her know he was there like any adult would. But he wanted

April to call him. She was the one who left. She should be the one to call. And because Judith would see him on the cameras, she should call him too.

But then, he thought, *she probably didn't have my cell.*

Calm down, Ron told himself. This was not a good way to start his apology to April. Because that was what he had come to town to do. Apologize and then bring April home.

If she wouldn't come with him, he'd have to adjust to what she wanted. In the meantime, he'd get some lunch, maybe walk through the old campus, and then go back to Judith's and wait for their return.

Ron didn't want to apologize over the phone. He wanted April to see that he meant it, that he loved her and couldn't live without her. And besides, what would the children say if they found out their mother had driven to Spring Falls without him?

He'd have to make sure they understood he had agreed to it, which meant he needed to get the simmering rage he felt under control and make himself believe this was what he wanted.

Control was something he practiced. He was proud that he could control himself and the world around him. But despite all his control over everything else, it was April he needed.

And if he couldn't control her, maybe he would have to adjust to what she needed so that they could be happy again. The idea didn't appeal to him, but he couldn't lose her.

In her car, Judith's Blink app from the camera buzzed. Yes, Ron had arrived. Just as she expected. However, she'd make sure that April had at least one day to herself before having to decide what to do about Ron.

Putting the phone away, she drove to her office, planning out what needed to be done that day because she had a feeling that things were about ready to move into new territories both in Spring Falls and in Pittsfield.

Marsha had called her about the woman coming to see them later that day. And she had agreed with Marsha that it would be wonderful if the woman named Grace brought grace with her, but neither of them expected that would be the case.

Yes, today was a pivotal day for everyone. But where it would take them was anyone's guess.

Thirty-Six

A few hours later, Marsha stood and stretched her back. It hurt where it always hurt. People would tell her it resulted from too much dance, and it was her fate, but she didn't accept that. Instead, she knew it resulted from not enough taking care of herself now.

Once she got settled in Spring Falls, she would start taking classes and get back into the world. Kill two birds with one stone. Maybe not dance, perhaps yoga. Maybe a gym. All possibilities.

For now, though, she rolled her head and then leaned over—first making sure no one could see her—and let herself drop into touching her toes, telling her back to let go.

Let go, good words to live by, she thought. Today was the day to let go of expectations of what she thought would happen, because she was sure none of it was what they expected.

One thing she knew for sure: she hoped never to have to look through old newspapers again. She was not a researcher. Nothing about the process interested her. It was only her desire to help Bree move through this part of her life and into the next that kept her going.

For hours she skimmed through pages and pages of microfiche, looking for the name Paul Stanford Mann or something involving a boy around the age he had been during that time. She didn't see anything with Paul's name, which didn't surprise her since they assumed he had changed his name.

There were fires, drunk driving incidents, and an alarming number of shootings. She printed the stories involving teenage boys, folded them, and stuffed them into her purse. Not because she thought she had found anything, but because she wanted something to show for all the time she had put in.

She found Cindy diligently looking through yearbooks upstairs, but Bree wasn't with her. Cindy smiled and said she had sent Bree to the reading lounge. Looking through yearbooks was not something Bree was handling well, making Cindy want to pull her hair out.

"Shall we just take her to Spring Falls and give up this search?" Cindy asked. "I don't think we are going to find out anything this way."

Since Bree couldn't hear them, Marsha told Cindy what Kathy had told her—that some woman was coming to meet them to give them more information about Paul.

"What? You mean we didn't have to be looking through all this stuff?"

"We had to keep Bree here. Besides, maybe this Grace person doesn't know the entire story, and what we found here could help."

"How long till she gets here?"

Marsha looked at her watch and said, "If we go to lunch and take our time, she should be here by then."

"God, I hope so. This sitting all day is not doing me any favors. Can we walk around the block a few times first, or take the long way to the restaurant to stretch our legs? I'm assuming you know where we're going?"

Marsha nodded and helped Cindy out of her seat. "Walking around the block a few times sounds like a great idea. We need to clear our heads anyway, and yes, Kathy told me where we could eat."

After collecting Bree, who had settled into a lounge chair with a book, and taking a few trips around the block, they found the restaurant Kathy suggested.

"After we eat, can we leave?" Bree asked. "I have decided that whatever Paul wanted me to know, I don't care about. If he really wanted me to know, he could have just come out and told me. And if he wanted me to get back to my life with the four of you, well, that's done now, too.

"Let's eat and then leave. If you want, we can stay the night, so we aren't too tired to drive, but I'm done."

"Sure," Marsha said, glancing at the clock on the wall and then at Cindy, who added, "Of course, Bree, whatever you want. But who knows, maybe after lunch, you'll feel like putting in another hour or two."

Bree laughed, "You think I am just tired and hungry, and I'll get over it, don't you?"

"Well...." Cindy said. "Now that you mention it."

Bree laughed again. "Well, it's possible I can stand another hour or two of searching for nothing after lunch."

"Perfect," Marsha said, glancing at her watch. Kathy should call soon to let them know Grace had arrived. With answers. Good or bad, at least they would know something.

Marsha's phone rang in the middle of sharing a tiramisu, and she stepped away from the table to answer it. A few minutes later, she was back with a smile on her face.

"That was Kathy. She said she had someone who might be able to help us."

"What? Kathy, the librarian, has someone who can help us? How does that make any sense?" Bree asked.

"Bree, let's wait and see what happens," Cindy said, reaching out to gently touch the back of Bree's hand. She knew Bree was not a fan of being touched, and she felt her jerk back the tiniest bit before relaxing.

Bree sighed. "Okay. But it's weird."

"Yep," Marsha answered. Yes, it was weird. All of it, and she expected it was going to get much weirder.

A few minutes later, Marsha stood and signaled to Kathy who was standing at the restaurant door looking for them. Trailing behind Kathy was a woman who looked like everyone's grandma was supposed to look.

She even looked like what she hoped a woman named Grace would look like. Slightly plump, shortish, dark gray hair, a string of pearls that competed with glasses on a chain, and a wide smile. Marsha couldn't help but smile back as they shook hands and invited her to sit down.

"Well, I'll be off," Kathy said. "Let me know if you need anything else, ladies."

Marsha promised herself she'd send Kathy a note of thanks and maybe a donation to the library when she got settled. Sometimes strangers were the best people. She had forgotten that. And now here was another total stranger who had made a long trip just to help them out.

Cindy asked Grace if she would like anything, and after getting her a coffee, they ordered another tiramisu so Grace could have some too.

Once Grace had taken a bite and declared it delicious, Bree couldn't wait one minute more.

"Who exactly are you, and why are you here?" she asked.

"Bree..." Cindy said.

"It's okay," Grace answered. "I understand. And I am as worried and nervous about being here as you are, Bree.

"Yes, I have some information for you about your husband because I knew him. A long time ago. And as you might have already figured out, his name was not Paul Stanford Mann."

Thirty-Seven

G race took another bite of the dessert, a sip of her coffee, before saying, "I used to live in Pittsfield. A long time ago, lifetimes, it feels like now.

"I was married to a man then who worked for a company that moved him around. And because I have always enjoyed change and adventure, it didn't bother me that we would move all the time. I enjoyed starting fresh and meeting new people.

"Through the years, I started to notice the same kinds of people everywhere, which meant I recognized what kind of people they were right away. I made friends quickly because of that and became a good listener and secret keeper if necessary.

"I learned to pay attention and notice things other people missed. All of which have served me well throughout my lifetime. I have learned that although there are evil people in this world—some I would call monsters—most people want to be good people.

"But good people do bad things too. Sometimes on purpose, but all too often by mistake."

Grace paused and looked at Bree, who had turned pale.

"Perhaps before I continue, do you want to go someplace more private?"

Bree nodded.

"After I tell you this story, I think you will want to stay in town to do a little more research. Do you think I could get a room where you're staying? Perhaps we could go there?"

While Cindy paid the bill, Marsha called the hotel, reserved a room for Grace, and switched her own room to a suite.

An hour later, they were all settled into chairs gathered around a coffee table in the small but cozy living room in Marsha's suite. Cindy had made a pot of coffee, and although they all had a cup in front of them, only Grace had taken a sip.

Trying to be as polite as possible, even though she felt like screaming, Bree looked at Grace and asked if she was ready to continue.

Grace smiled at Bree, feeling Bree's tension and fear, knowing she would make it worse before she could make it better.

"As I was saying, good people do bad things. Sometimes intentionally, often not. Then there is a cascade of events that can happen, often making things much worse. When that happens, we all face the same questions. Do I tell what I did? Do I try to make it right? Or do I hope that no one ever finds out?

"All these decisions impact people's lives forever, but at the moment, most of us don't realize it. I am sure you all have done things you regretted. Hurt people you didn't mean to hurt. And maybe you made it worse based on what you did trying to fix it. It's what humans do, isn't it?

"But we always have a chance to try and make it right later. Perhaps how we do it is not the wisest way, but I believe that the intent behind it makes a difference."

"Are you telling me my husband did something bad, and then what he did afterward made it worse, and now that he's dead and since he didn't face it, he is making me do it?

"That's what you are saying, isn't it? You want me to understand, so I'll forgive him for what he did? How horrible was it? No, I don't think I want to know."

Bree stood and walked out the door, letting it slam behind her. Cindy moved to go after her, but Grace said, "Let her go. She'll be back. That woman has courage and curiosity. Both of them will win out."

"While she's gone, perhaps tell me a little about yourselves and how you met?"

By the time Cindy had told the story of how Bree had found her in the cloakroom and how Bree found Marsha in a dance class, and then a little about April and Judith back in Spring Falls, Bree had returned.

All three women smiled at her, and Marsha said, "We've been telling Grace about how we all met. And how you kept us all together and protected us while we were in school."

"We were just getting to the part where you saw Paul and said you were going to marry him," Cindy added, then blushed, thinking that might not have been something Bree wanted to talk about.

"Did I?" Bree asked. "Did I protect you?"

Marsha nodded. "You did. You constantly reminded us to stick together. Judith scared people, Cindy made everyone feel safe. April made people laugh. I kept you all wondering where I was and when would I get there. But you, Bree, you were the rock we made our life around."

"And then I left," Bree said. "And you all remained for each other."

Looking at Grace, Bree asked, "Is this what you mean by good people making wrong choices?"

"Maybe it wasn't a wrong choice at the time, Bree," Grace answered. "But it is an example of how we have to make choices based on what we think is right in the middle of very emotional and trying times."

"And that's what Paul did? He did something wrong and made a choice that he wants me to fix?"

"I believe so," Grace answered. "Are you willing?"

"Do I have a choice?" Bree said. "If I don't find out what he did and then do whatever I can to make it right, then I am consciously doing something bad. Well, maybe not bad, but definitely not right. I don't think I can live with that.

"And I am mad at Paul for making me deal with this now. Is that wrong?"

"I think we can be mad at people and still love them," Grace answered. "Perhaps finding out will help you understand him better."

"So this last gift crap wasn't a last gift to me. It's a last gift to himself."

Bree wanted to kick something she was so mad, but at least she didn't feel dead inside anymore. She could pretend that's what Paul wanted to give her, enough anger to get her moving again. Well, if that's the case, it was working.

"I'm ready for the story, Grace. But first, I am curious. Are you here to tell me this because you are trying to make up for something that you did that was bad?"

Grace smiled at Bree. "What a wise question to ask, and yes, I too made a decision, and I have never been sure whether it was the right one or the wrong one. The man you knew as Paul is giving me this gift too. A chance to make things right, or at least better."

It was Marsha who asked, "So his name wasn't Paul Stanford Mann?"

"No, my dear, it wasn't. His name was Stan Joseph Ford."

Marsha gasped, reached into her purse for the papers she printed out at the library, shuffled through them, and then handed one to Grace.

"Is this who he was and what he did?"

Thirty-Eight

April spent the morning exploring what had stayed the same and what had changed on Main Street in Spring Falls. She had lunch at a tiny restaurant run by one of Mimi and Janet's friends and declared both the food and the adventure of trying something new as delicious and satisfying.

After lunch, watching Mimi and Janet as they worked with customers that walked in the door while running an online business made April tingle with excitement. Was this something she could do? Was she too old to learn?

Both Mimi and Janet burst out laughing when she asked that question. "Old? What's too old?" Janet said. "Some people might say that we are too young to be doing this!"

"Age means nothing anymore," Mimi added. "It's just an excuse people use. If you like this business, we could use help while Cindy is away. Besides, wouldn't it be great for her to find out that one of her best friends wants to learn how to help her?"

"Well, if you put it that way." April laughed. "But I think I need a new look."

When Mimi and Janet exchanged looks, April knew she was right.

"Can you help me?"

"Today?" Mimi asked.

April nodded. There was a timeline going on in her head. Ron hadn't contacted her, but she knew him. He would never just let things be. He'd be waiting for her to apologize. If she didn't go back, eventually he'd come to get her. And then he would want her to go home with him and back to the life they had built.

But the brief moments of freedom she felt walking the streets and watching Mimi and Janet had given her courage.

She wouldn't leave Ron, but she had to start living a life for herself. Hopefully, he'd understand. And what would tell him all of this without words was if she transformed herself as much as possible before she saw him again.

"I'll call my hairdresser, tell him it's an emergency," Mimi said.

"And I'll take you shopping if Mimi can handle the gallery by herself for an hour."

Mimi nodded her consent while explaining to her hairdresser what she needed.

"Wow, you must be living under a lucky star or something. He said the customer who was supposed to be there right now canceled at the last minute. He can take you now—if you hurry!"

"I'll take you," Janet said, "And pick you up when you're done, and we'll get you some clothes."

"I'll never be able to thank you enough," April said.

"Oh, we'll give you lots of ways! But now, get your butt out of here," Mimi said.

Janet grabbed April's arm, and the two of them rushed out the back door, but then April turned and rushed back to Mimi and, standing on her tiptoes, hugged her, surprising them both.

Mimi stared after April in wonder. When Judith brought April in that morning, she did not know that this woman would hug her just like her mother used to hug her. Tears pooled in her eyes, and she wiped them away as a couple came through the door heading for the wall of paintings by one of their local artists.

Mimi knew the artist, knew she was struggling at the moment, and a sale would be a godsend. Maybe this was her day to make people happy—both the artist and the couple who had stopped in front of one of her favorite paintings.

Three hours later, the sale made to the couple, and another online, Janet flew in the back door all smiles.

"Are you ready?" she called out.

"Bring it on!" Mimi responded.

Janet opened the back door, and a beautiful woman entered. Her hair, styled into soft, shiny curls on the top of her head and cut short on the side, made her look ten years younger. She was wearing a flowered dress with a jean jacket and short blue boots with a stacked heel.

"Who are you" Mimi squealed.

"I am not sure who I am," April said. "But I know you are my fairy godmothers. I feel like a brand new woman."

"And you look like one too!" Judith said, coming in behind her. "What have you done with the woman who showed up at my house last night?"

"Oh, I think she is still there, but this will give me the courage to be someone new."

As Judith hugged her friend, she mouthed thank you over April's shoulder to Mimi and Janet. Then she stepped back, holding April by the shoulders, and said, "Well, this deserves a nice dinner at my favorite restaurant."

"Should I stay and help close up?" April asked.

"You go ahead. You are just watching today. We'll put you to work tomorrow," Janet said, surprised at the catch in her throat. She'd only met this woman a few hours before but already felt connected to her.

"Where are we going to eat?"

"A place called ParaTi. It's not too fancy, but great food, and perhaps my favorite waitress will be there so you can meet her."

"Sounds like a party," April giggled.

Judith laughed, "You're already speaking Spring Falls lingo again. But I understand the owner meant it to mean 'For You.'"

"Oops," April laughed. "But then, that's still a party!"

Neither April nor Judith saw Ron sitting in his car across the street. He knew Cindy owned an art gallery, and he wanted to stop by and see what it looked like. Part of his day of relearning the town. It had surprised him how much he enjoyed it and thought that perhaps if April wanted to stay in town for a while, it would be okay with him.

He planned to go over to Judith's when he knew she and April would be there and surprise them. He had not expected to see Judith there with some woman, and he wondered where April was.

It was only when he heard them laughing that he realized that the woman with Judith was April. A transformed April. One who reminded him of the April he had met so many years before.

Gripping the steering wheel, he watched as they drove away. April had done all that in a day. Was he losing her?

No matter what, he told himself, *I can't let that happen.*

Thirty-Nine

"Yes, that's it," Grace said. "Or at least the newspaper version of what happened. Of course, it was so much more than that."

Marsha had passed the article around so everyone could read it. It was dated June 1974. The headline read, "Drunk Driver Kills Local Couple."

Grace waited until all the women read the article. It was brief, barely mentioning the couple who died.

People deserve more respect than this, Bree thought.

The article concentrated mostly on the drunk driver. He had crossed the median and driven straight into the oncoming car. The couple in the front seat were killed on impact. Their fourteen-year-old son, Stan, and a friend in the back seat survived.

"This is the secret?" Bree cried. "It's horrible. I can see why Paul—I refuse to call him Stan—didn't want to talk about it. But keep it a secret? I don't understand. And why would he change his name over this?"

"Maybe he was trying to make a new name for himself?" Marsha asked both Bree and Grace, hoping that was the only reason.

"That was the end result, but not the reason," Grace said. "It was the guilt."

"Guilt?" Cindy said. "How could a fourteen-year-old boy be responsible for a drunk driver?"

Grace sighed. "Well, he wasn't, of course, but he thought he was."

Everyone waited for Grace to say more, but when she didn't, Bree asked, "Grace, we need to know what happened. Why not start with how you got involved with whatever this is about."

Grace nodded and, sitting up straighter, continued the story.

"I was working as a volunteer aide at the hospital, which is how I met Paul. He wouldn't speak to anyone, just stared at the ceiling. Sometimes he'd start screaming that it was all his fault. The nurses and doctors were trying to decide how safe it was to give him more sedatives.

"One nurse knew me and asked if I would be willing to sit with him. His parents were all he had. They tried to find other family members for him, but they had been unsuccessful."

All the women listening were fighting back their tears. Bree was doing her best not to collapse into a fit of sobbing. How could she have been mad at him for feeling guilty?

"Was it all about him thinking he had caused the wreck? But why would he?" Marsha asked.

Grace nodded. "Yes, and it was terrible to hear him scream and cry about it after the shock had worn off. No one could figure out why he kept saying it was his fault. A drunk driver coming the other way had turned into their lane and ran directly into them. No one could have done anything to stop him.

"The driver confessed it was entirely his fault. He had been out drinking and thought he could get home safely. He was severely injured but didn't die, and I believe he went to jail for a time after that since it wasn't his first drunk driving charge and people died.

"After hearing the story, I was grateful that I could do something, and I sat in Stan's room all day and into the night, just taking small breaks for food. The following day, Stan—sorry, Paul—asked me who I was and why I was there.

"It was the first sentence he had said other than saying it was his fault, and I was overjoyed, but tried not to show it. I told him my name and said I was there if he needed anything. He turned his head away from me and said he needed nothing. And he wouldn't ever again.

"That was so obviously untrue that I stayed that day and the next. He rarely spoke, but at least he seemed more comfortable with my being there and was no longer screaming uncontrollably.

"Normally he would have been released from the hospital, but since they still hadn't found relatives, they were keeping him there until they could figure out what to do with him.

"Seeing him lie there with nowhere to go broke my heart. My nurse friend somehow arranged for my husband and me to take him home to recuperate while the authorities continued to hunt for relatives.

"That night he woke up screaming and finally broke down and told us the whole story about the wreck and why he believed it to be his fault. And what he had done afterward that made it worse.

"He told us that right before the accident, he was arguing with his father. 'Acting like a brat as always,' he said.

"His mother was crying, his dad was yelling, and he was yelling back. Suddenly, there was a car coming straight at them. He could remember his mother screaming, and then he blacked out.

"When he woke, he saw the front of the car squashed up against his parents and blood covering everything. All he could think about was how it was his fault that it had happened, and he had to get away.

"He didn't even think about the woman in the back seat with him, didn't even look her way, he told me. Instead, he fell out of the car, crawled along the highway until he reached the side of the road, and then started running.

"Where were you going?" I asked him.

"Away where no one would ever find me," he said.

As Grace told the story, Bree started to shake. Marsha put a blanket around her, brought her a water glass, and made her drink.

"Shall I continue?" Grace asked.

"Yes," Bree answered. "I need to know. We all need to know."

"The police told me they found him hours later in the woods by the highway, in shock, with a broken arm and a concussion. He kept screaming and crying that it was all his fault, begging them not to help him, saying he just wanted to die.

"The authorities let Paul stay with us as temporary foster parents until they could place him somewhere else, which was a blessing for all of us. I helped him plan a small funeral.

"It was only him and us and my friend from the hospital, but I think it helped to have a small amount of closure for him. But after that, he still didn't want to see anyone and hid away in his room most of the day.

"Because it was almost the end of the school year, everyone involved agreed he didn't have to go back to school. My husband was always working, so it was just Paul and me at home most days.

"After a time, he started talking and asked me to help him decide what to do next, probably because he couldn't figure out who else to ask."

Grace stopped and took a sip of her now-cold coffee before continuing.

"All this is just a sad story. However, I know it doesn't explain how he ended up in Spring Falls, with a changed name, or my part in what he kept a secret."

Grace picked up the article where Bree had laid it on the coffee table.

"There is something wrong with this article," Grace said, smoothing it out on her lap. "The reason why he wanted to become someone else, and why I helped him to do it. What they don't say is that there was another person who died that day."

Forty

"The woman in the back seat?" Cindy asked. "She died?"

"No, not her. Although she was injured, she didn't die. She was pregnant. It was her baby that died. That was where they were going, to the hospital.

"Nora Gray was a next-door neighbor whose husband was in the military, stationed overseas in Vietnam. They had worried that he wouldn't be able to get leave, so they had already arranged that Paul's parents would take her, just in case. So when the baby started coming early, they were ready.

"Paul knew her well. She was kind and gentle, and he considered her not only a friend but another parent when he needed one. He was quite the nerd when being a quiet, nerdy boy didn't make you popular. Which meant he struggled in school and with people's expectations. He felt understood by Nora.

"This is all something he told me later. How much he loved her, how much Nora had stood by him when he needed it. That was what was eating him up. He had run away, and then her baby died.

"Nora called the house asking to see Paul more than once, but he refused to see her. He told me he couldn't face her. The baby died, and it was his fault."

"Because he believed he caused the wreck?" Cindy asked.

"Yes, and then because he ran away. He believed that the baby would have lived if he had stayed with her. But instead, he ran. The ambulance was at the scene of the wreck almost immediately, so really, if they could have saved the baby, they would have done it. That's what Nora wanted him to know, that it wasn't his fault.

"However, in Paul's mind, everyone in town knew him as a murderer. He pleaded with me to help him be someone else. And that's what I did. I helped him.

"We found a couple who would be his foster family, and we changed his name. Within a few months, he was gone. He asked me to let him be, let him have another life, and tell no one what happened to him. I always wondered if running away again was the right thing for him to do.

"But he had asked me to never contact him. He wanted to be free of his past. That, too, is something I wonder if I did right. Was a fourteen-year-old boy making a good decision? But I did what he asked. Every time I thought of him, I would pray that he found happiness.

"Now, looking at you, Bree, I see he did, and perhaps that means I did the right thing. He made a life for himself, one that he deserved."

Bree stood up, the blanket dropping to the floor, and gave the other women in the room what Marsha called her 'look.'

"Well, there must be more to this story because if that's all that happened, tragic as it was, I believe that eventually, he would have told me. There has to be more to it."

Taking a deep breath, Bree said, "And I am going to find out what it is. Can we find Nora Gray? Maybe she can help find out what else he was hiding. Because I am sure that Paul was hiding something, and I need to know."

"That was over forty-five years ago, Bree," Grace said. "She might be hard to find."

"How old was she then?"

"In her late twenties."

"Well, then, she could still be around, couldn't she?

Cindy got up and got her computer and turned it on. "Well, we know her name. And now that we know how all this began—with an accident and a boy named Stan Joseph Ford—we can get Judith on this. She'll know how to find out more."

A few minutes later, she said, "Okay, done. I told her what we know and asked her to get help. She's at dinner with April, so she said she'd contact her "guy" and have him get started.

"Oh, and she said to check our phones, she sent us a picture."

"Wow," Marsha said. "Look at April!"

She showed the picture of their other two friends to Grace and then asked her if she would take a picture of the three of them.

After the photos were exchanged, it was Marsha who said, "That's all we can do tonight. Let's get some rest. Perhaps by morning, we'll have something to go on to find this mystery woman and get more answers."

A few minutes later, after Grace said goodnight to Cindy and Bree, she closed the door of her room and leaned against it, exhausted but relieved of a burden she had carried for too many years.

She would never have imagined she'd be back again when she left this town years before, but she was glad that she was. And although she had told what she knew, there was still work to do. This was a story with a loose ending, and for Paul's sake, she would help close the loop.

Grace only hoped that it brought peace to his wife in doing so. Perhaps that was what Paul meant when he said it was his last gift. By giving her a chance to tell someone, he had given her a last gift, too. Because Grace knew that sometimes the dead stay around until what they left undone is completed, she whispered her thanks to Paul, hoping he was listening.

As she snuggled down into bed, she thought about how grateful she was to be given this chance to help Bree. But she couldn't wait to head home and resume her life in Doveland.

However, first, she had to make sure she had done everything she could to finish what she and Paul had started so many years before.

Forty-One

His phone kept ringing, and Bruce cursed at himself for forgetting to turn the sound off when he went to bed. But it had been a day full of appointments, and each one seemed more challenging than the last, until finally he broke down and told his secretary to limit how many people came in each day from now on. Something he never thought he would do.

She had given him a look, which meant "you should have told me before, but hey, people need you, so maybe this is not a good idea."

Then she sighed and said, "Okay, but it will take a few weeks before the ones I've already booked thin out." Then, seeing his exhaustion, she softened and added, "But when they cancel, I won't book someone in their place."

He had come home, stripped off his clothes, and fallen asleep within minutes. And now the phone was ringing? Who would call him at this time of the night? Opening one eye, Bruce saw it was not night. It was morning, sorta. Six in the morning, to be exact.

Still, who would be calling him this early? Finally, the phone stopped ringing, and the voice mail beeped instead. Not many people had Bruce's mobile phone number. Only his secretary, his family, and a few close friends. Rolling over to find the phone, he felt a frisson of fear that something was wrong, but when he saw who had called, that fear turned to something else. He wasn't sure exactly what that something else was, but he knew it meant trouble for him.

Not dealing with it now, he mumbled to himself, rolled over away from the phone, punched his pillow to fluff it up the right way, and tried to go back to sleep. But the deep cocooning sleep he had fallen into last night refused to come back.

Swearing to himself, he stumbled out of bed to the shower. First really hot, then cold. Well, not cold exactly, but he was getting there. At first, he had hated the cold shower part, but now he enjoyed it. Besides, he noticed that the actual cold of the Pennsylvania winter had not bothered him as much as it did before, so it must be doing something. If it meant he was more in charge of what he believed and more open to change, then he accepted it as a good thing.

Standing at his kitchen counter, drinking his first cup of coffee, Bruce looked out the window to his tiny backyard. Last year he had taken up gardening, mainly to calm himself after a stressful day, and now he could see that his work had paid off.

Stress was not something he thought he would feel being an estate attorney. He wanted to feel helpful. He wanted to feel that he had done something that made people's lives better. First, by helping the ones who planned their estates before their death. Relieving them of the stress they carried, hoping that they were doing the right thing, or at least something that made their loved ones' lives easier, felt good. That part was a joy—most of the time.

The hard part was on the other side of it. Bruce was always the person called after a loved one died. It was his job to make resolving the estate as painless as possible. The people in grief he could understand, and he did his best to comfort them. But there were always people who came in angry and wanted to contest what his clients had requested.

Those were the people that drove him crazy and made him think about quitting. Or at least slowing down. Or taking an extended vacation and maybe never returning. He had worked his entire life to build a respectable business, and now that he had, he wasn't sure it was what he wanted anymore.

How did you get here, Bruce, he asked himself. He had built the life he wanted, minus a wife, although to be totally honest with himself, he had never wanted a wife. Other people wanted it for him. There had been someone in college, but she had chosen someone else, and after that, the desire to find love had left him.

And when he was honest with himself, he knew that he only had pursued her because that was what was expected of him. He was very grateful that she had been wise enough to pick someone much better for her than him.

He loved his solitary life. The people he saw during the day were enough people for him. However, for years, people had tried to match him up with someone. Sometimes blatantly, and sometimes they tried to trick him into meeting someone. He was often touted as the most eligible bachelor in town, which he hated. People still tried to match him up once in a while, but his friends had learned their lesson. Let him be. He was happy.

When he was a boy, he went along with all the other boys, who were always talking about girls and trying to convince them to go to bed with them. But he only did it because even his friends would have beaten the crap out of him for not being like them.

Once he admitted to himself that he didn't want what his friends wanted and didn't experience what they seemed to experience about relations, Bruce decided something was wrong with him. Dating wasn't something he enjoyed or needed. But Bruce kept his worries to himself, fearing what that meant. It was his secret, one he barely shared with himself.

And then, one day, he stumbled across an article about people who were asexual. Just seeing the word changed his world. He understood for the first time what people meant when they said everything fell into place when they discovered they were gay or trans. It was a relief to put a word to it. It was a brief article, but it described his feelings exactly. He wasn't a freak. It wasn't a bad thing. Just different.

That night, he read the article again and then put his head into his hands and cried. Putting a name to how he felt didn't change his outside world, but it changed his internal one. He was at peace with himself.

But now, there was this problem that Paul Mann had started. Not only the letters, not only the package he still had in his safe waiting for the question that would bring it out. But the woman named Judith. She was a problem.

Maybe not. Maybe I am making something out of nothing, Bruce said to himself and finally picked up the phone to listen to the voice mail she had left. He sighed in relief. She only wanted some information, and he could give her that without actually looking at her again. But the fact that he had given her his mobile number worried him. What was he thinking?

He couldn't wait until this was all over and he could go back to the life he had worked so hard to build. Feelings he hadn't had since college would not tear it down. Not if he had anything to say about it.

Forty-Two

They met the next morning in Marsha's room, as agreed. Marsha had barely slept, which meant she had time to walk to the nearest coffee shop and bring back everyone's favorite coffee and pastry. She had to guess what Grace would like and realized how little they knew about her.

So when Grace arrived first, Marsha prompted her to tell her a little about her life. She learned that Grace lived in what she called a magical town with fantastic friends who shared strange but lovely adventures. She owned a coffee shop that sold books.

"A dream come true," Grace said.

"The coffee shop?"

"All of it. I'm living the life I wanted and spent my entire life preparing to live."

Marsha didn't have a chance to ask her more questions because as soon as Bree and Cindy came in the door, all attention went to them. Cindy looked as if she was the cat who ate a mouse, and Bree was looking more like the Bree they used to know. She was still pale, too thin, but now, instead of grief and anger radiating from her, there was determination.

Bree pointed at Cindy and said, "She wouldn't tell me a thing until we all got together."

Cindy laughed, "Well, I didn't want to have to say it twice, that's all."

"What did you find?" Marsha asked, motioning for everyone to get a coffee and pastry and sit down.

"Mmm," Cindy said, taking a bite of her blueberry muffin. "You remembered!"

Marsha smiled and ducked her head. She couldn't believe that those simple words made her want to cry.

"Cindy!" Bree said. "Please!"

Taking a sip of coffee to wash the muffin down, Cindy paused and, with a huge smile on her face, said, "I found her. Well, I didn't find her. Judith did. I guess it wasn't all that hard. But you know Judith enjoys doing these things."

"Cindy!" Bree said again.

"Sorry, I just didn't know how much I would love solving these little mysteries. So here's what Judith said. As we knew, at the time of the accident, her name was Nora Gray. What we didn't know was her husband's name was Paul."

"Oh," Bree said, her eyes welling up with tears.

"Now I remember," Grace said. "That's why Stan wanted to be called Paul. He said it meant he would never forget what he had done."

"So you mean, every time someone called him Paul, it reminded him of the accident, and yet he kept it a secret? He was punishing himself all these years?" Bree said, her voice catching. "How could I not have seen it?"

Grace reached out and held Bree's hand, and to everyone's surprise, Bree let her.

Cindy cleared her throat, trying not to cry now that she realized what Paul had done. Before, it was just a mystery to solve. Now, it was about someone's guilt and unnecessary pain.

"So, yes, Nora and Paul Gray. However, Paul died in the war, and Nora disappeared after that. Judith thinks she moved around, perhaps changed her name, because Judith couldn't find anything about her during that time. At least not now. It would take longer, but that's okay. Because a few years ago, Nora popped up again in Pittsfield with a different name. Now she is Noreen Ferguson. And, here's the great news: I have her address!"

No one said anything, waiting to see what Bree would say.

"Why?" Bree said.

"Why, what dear?" Grace asked.

"Why go see her? We know Paul's secret now. What else is there to know? I thought about this all night. I found out his secret, and if there is another one, why do I want to know it?"

"Do you think this is what Paul sent you to find out? Only what I told you? That's the secret?" Grace asked.

"Well, why not? It's big enough, isn't it? And if I think that the gift he wanted to give me was to stop feeling sorry for myself and go back to the Ruby Sisters, well, he did that. And I am grateful. Upset at him for keeping it from me, but I'll get over it."

"And that's enough? Aren't you curious to know if there is more?" Grace asked, holding both of Bree's hands and looking at her so Bree couldn't look away.

"Maybe," Bree finally said, sighing. "Okay, yes. It feels as if there is more. Maybe we should find out what this Nora can tell us about what happened. Maybe he wanted closure for her, too."

Marsha let go of the breath she didn't realize she was holding, as did Cindy. Both of them knew there had to be more. Maybe Bree was right. It was only to tell Nora what happened to Paul and have her meet Bree. On the other hand, neither of them thought Paul had sent them on this trip just to find out about the accident that changed his life at fourteen.

"I'll drive," Marsha said.

An hour later, everyone piled into Marsha's car. Cindy sat in the front seat so she could help with directions.

"What did Nora do for a living?" Bree asked Grace, thinking it would give them something to talk about once they met her. How weird was it they were just going to drive up to her house and knock on her door and introduce themselves?

"She taught elementary school when I knew her. But I don't know what she did afterward."

"I guess she stayed off the internet since Judith couldn't find her that way. Maybe she was hiding. Or maybe she just doesn't like it," Cindy said.

"I can understand that," Grace laughed. "Although I got my smartphone, I don't really use it for anything other than a phone."

Twenty minutes later, they pulled up in front of the address that Judith had given them. The house's yard looked well cared for, even though the place looked as if it had seen better days and needed repairs.

"Maybe she's not up yet?" Cindy asked, seeing all the closed blinds and no lights on through the windows.

"Well, we can't just sit out here like stalkers," Bree said, getting out of the car and heading up the tiny sidewalk. The others joined her, being careful as they went up the crumbling steps to the front porch.

There was one chair on the porch with a small round metal table beside it, and Marsha thought she saw what her future might have looked like if she hadn't returned to her friends.

Bree knocked on the door and rang the doorbell, but there was no movement inside.

"Are you looking for Noreen?" A woman standing in the yard next door asked.

Bree walked down the steps and over to the woman before answering. "Yes. Are we too early for her?"

"I'm sorry," the woman said, "You're not too early. You are actually too late. Noreen passed away."

Forty-Three

"I'm sorry. Did you know Noreen?" the neighbor asked, seeing Bree's face grow even paler.

Bree shook her head and then gestured at Grace, who answered. "I did, briefly, a long time ago. I thought I would check in with her while I was in town."

Hearing that Nora was dead was a blow that Bree wasn't expecting. Only then did she realize how much she hoped there was more to the mystery, even though she kept denying that to herself. Now, they would never know, and she felt deeply disappointed.

"I wish I could tell you more, but Noreen had moved here only a few months before she died, and I didn't get to know her. I tried, but she obviously just wanted to be left alone. In fact, Noreen called the ambulance herself, and then she never came home."

Bree had sat down on the porch steps and was barely listening, so it was Grace who kept asking the questions.

"Do you know if she owned this house?"

"No. It's a rental. Noreen's stuff is still inside because the owner lives out of town and hasn't come by to clean it out yet."

Looking at Bree sitting on the steps, she added, "Is there anything I can do for you?"

"Thank you, but no. I think it's all over now."

Grace thanked the neighbor for her kindness and took Bree's hand as they walked back to the car. Cindy stayed behind for a moment and then handed the neighbor her card. If you remember anything else, would you call me?

"Will she be okay?"

"In time."

Back in the car, Marsha asked, "Now what?"

"Food," Cindy said. "Before we do anything, I need more food."

Marsha smiled at Cindy. Marsha knew what Cindy was trying to do and was grateful because, at the moment, it looked as if it was all over. She felt a huge letdown, and she knew everyone else did too. She didn't know what she had expected, but it wasn't this.

Cindy found an Italian restaurant nearby and guided them to it. After everyone had ordered, Grace, Marsha, and Cindy kept up a running conversation, talking about almost anything except why they were there in the first place.

During one of her visits to the table to fill their water glasses, the waitress heard Cindy say that it was too bad they didn't know where Paul's parents were buried because if they did, they could pay their respects before leaving town.

"That's a good idea. And I do know where," Grace said. "However, I only remember the cemetery, but not where their graves are. That was a long time ago."

The waitress said, "Sorry for listening in, but you can go online and look."

"Now, this is why I need to use my phone more," Grace laughed. "Thanks for telling us."

Cindy googled the website and then said, "Okay, what were their names?"

Marsha pulled out the article about the crash and said, "Joseph and Maureen Ford."

It took Cindy only a few minutes before she cried out, "Found them!"

"Well, then, let's eat up and go visit some dead people," Marsha said, raising her glass.

Cindy sucked in her breath as Grace turned to look at Bree, who had turned pale again.

"What? It's true." Marsha said. "They are dead. None of us knew them. It's time to go meet them, right?"

"Right," Cindy said, once again trying to lighten the mood.

Bree stayed silent, but Grace added, "It's a good idea. After all, we're here. It's Paul's parents, and probably no one has visited them since Paul left town.

"I know I didn't. My husband and I moved on, again, not long after all this happened, and they had no other family."

"Do you think they'll know that we are there?" Marsha asked Grace.

"I think that there is much that we don't know, so who can say? I know that what we see and know of this world is minuscule compared to what else is going on. So why not? It can't hurt anything, and it just might help."

Grace reached over and squeezed Bree's hand, and Bree gave her a little smile back and said, "Why not?"

Forty-Four

B ree went along with the plan, not caring what they did next. For her, at this moment, life was just one big blank open sucking hole, and she didn't see how visiting graves of dead people she had never met would help. She didn't know them. She would never know them. Why bother? All she felt was numb.

But her friends wanted to go, and it was the least she could do for them. Besides, she was stuck in Marsha's car. She hated not being in charge of where she wanted to go, when she wanted to go. The sooner she got back to living her life, the better.

After they stopped at a local florist to get flowers, Cindy directed them to the cemetery, reading aloud what she found out about it from their website. It had been around since 1842 and was now funded entirely by donations.

"There are some interesting people buried here," Cindy said, "Including civil war soldiers."

As Cindy explained more about who was buried there besides Paul's parents, Grace thought about her friends back home in Doveland. If Bryan were here, he would see all the in-betweeners, people who hadn't yet learned they were dead or had unfinished

217

business, and some of them would ask him for help. And being Bryan, he would say yes, because that's what he did. She missed him. She missed Doveland.

I've done what Paul wanted me to do, she thought. After they finished at the cemetery, she would be ready to go home.

"It's beautiful," Marsha breathed. Everyone nodded, including Bree. The air was sweet with May flowers, and birds sang in the trees. She hadn't expected it to be such a peaceful place.

Watching the cemetery map she had on her phone, Cindy led them through the graves until they found the two simple markers. Bree laid the flowers on their graves and thanked them for bringing their son into the world.

"He was a good man," Bree said to Joseph and Maureen. "I know he kept this secret, but he thought it was the right thing to do."

As Bree said those words, she felt her spirit lighten as she realized that it was true. He had thought it was the right thing to do, and he had been a good man and husband to her. Perhaps it was time to forgive him for leaving her.

Besides, the two of them had a secret together, too. And she had no plans for telling anyone about it. Ever. Remembering the secret that they shared, she forgave Paul a little more. He had kept what happened to him at fourteen a secret, but he had also kept what happened to her a secret.

"I loved—love—your son," she told the Fords as tears ran down her face. It was true. She did. From the moment she saw him, she loved him, and she would love him forever.

"I'm sorry, Paul," she whispered to the wind, hoping he would hear her.

Turning to her friends who had stepped away while she visited Paul's parents, she asked Cindy if perhaps Noreen Ferguson was buried there too.

"Why didn't I think of that?" Cindy asked, checking her phone. "Yes, just a few rows over!"

Bree took a few sprigs of flowers from the ones she had put on the Ford's grave, and they made their way over to Noreen's.

It was a newer headstone and easy to read, "Noreen Ferguson. A beloved mother."

"I'm sorry," Bree said to Noreen, even though she knew Nora couldn't hear her. "He loved you too, and of course, he didn't mean for your baby to die."

"I guess Paul arranged for this," Marsha said, gesturing at the headstone. "It was part of his last gift to her, too."

Bree nodded. "He was a good man, wasn't he?"

All three women stood in a circle around Bree and said, "Yes, Bree, he was."

Back at the hotel, Grace told them it was time for her to leave. She would drive for a few hours, stop at a motel for the night, and be home by noon the next day.

Once again, all four women gathered together in a group hug, but this time around Grace, thanking her for bringing them the information they needed.

Before Grace left, she pulled Bree away from the group and said, "I know how hard it is to lose someone you love as much as you loved Paul. But you have to know that his life continues, and someday you will see him again. So make a good life for yourself while you are here because that is what he would want. You know that, don't you?"

Bree nodded, tears running down her face, and gave Grace one last hug.

The three friends waved as Grace drove away, and then Bree turned to her friends. "Cindy, do you mind riding with Marsha back to Spring Falls?"

"Of course not, but why?"

"I'm leaving too."

"Now?" Cindy squeaked.

"Now. Could we say goodbye now, please? I don't want to cry in front of the whole world. I just need some time to myself."

Both women looked shocked, and Cindy started to cry.

"Please understand," Bree said. "I promise I'll come to Spring Falls. Besides, you have that dang Find Me app on your phones. You'll know I'm okay."

"You promise?" Cindy asked.

"I promise," Bree said, reaching out and hugging Cindy. "Thank you for coming and getting me out of my funk. If you hadn't come, I might still be sitting against the door sobbing. You rescued me. You both rescued me. I will not forget that, ever!"

"Paul's gift to all of us, reuniting the Ruby Sisters," Marsha said.

Sniffing, Cindy said, "Okay. We'll see you soon. Get your stuff. We'll wait right here and wave goodbye. Just promise you'll be okay."

"I promise," Bree said again. "I just have some thinking to do."

A few minutes later, Bree was back with her luggage, and Marsha handed her a bag filled with snacks and a cold pack filled with sodas.

Bree took it, trying not to cry, knowing Marsha had rushed into the hotel's store to get all of it before she left.

"Ruby Sisters forever," she whispered.

She didn't look back, but she knew they were standing there watching her go, and they would be there when she was ready to see them again. But she needed to think about how she would start her life over, and she needed to do that by herself.

Forty-Five

B y the time Bruce got to his office, Judith had called at least two more times. He had ignored all her calls. He would talk when he was good and ready. Of course, he wasn't sure he would ever be ready for that woman.

However, he had an obligation to Paul to fulfill his last wish. Not for the first, or the last time, he wished he had never agreed to such a ridiculous thing to do. Besides, the look his secretary gave him told him that Judith had called her too, and it was not good to piss off his secretary. It was time to take care of Judith.

Closing his office door, he swiveled to look out the window at the apple tree, asked it to give him a little help, and punched in her number. It rang and went to voice mail.

"Ah, we're playing that game," Bruce said to the tree, and the tree ruffled in the wind in response.

Bruce left a message saying he was returning her call and turned to the paperwork on his desk. A few minutes later, his secretary told him that Judith was on the line, and he picked it up with a cheery hello and was startled when he realized he did feel cheery hearing her voice.

Except her first words were, "Avoiding me? Too busy to deal with this mess your client made?"

"Yes, no, I mean, no, I am not avoiding you, and yes, I am busy. But what mess?"

Bruce gritted his teeth, worried about what she would say next. He wasn't ready to deal with all of it right now. Because, as Judith said, it was a mess. But not one she could know about. Yet.

On the other end of the phone, Judith was silent. He waited.

"Sorry. I was taking out on you things that have nothing to do with Paul and his ridiculous last gift crap."

"Not a fan, I gather."

"Well, truthfully, that's a yes and no answer, too. But more yes than no, I guess. Good grief, this is ridiculous. I'm not sure why I am even bothering you with this."

"No bother," Bruce answered, meaning it. "But why all the calls? What's up that I can help you with?"

Again, Judith was silent on the other end, and he waited.

"Honestly, I don't know why I called. Maybe to find out what else you can tell me about Paul's plans, so I can prepare for them. I'm not used to not knowing. It's my job to know. And I don't.

"Was Paul's plan only to get Bree back out into the world and reunite the Ruby Sisters? If that was it, it has worked. Mostly. And, did you know about his name change and why he did it?"

Bruce sighed. "Well, now that you know, I can answer that. Yes, I did. He had to tell me so I could make sure his wishes couldn't be contested. He changed his name legally, but he didn't want to leave any loopholes."

"But is there more? It feels as if there is more."

"You know I can't tell you that, Judith. Client attorney privilege."

"Which means there's more, doesn't it?" Judith demanded.

"Look, I can't help you by telling you more, but I can listen to what's happening now. Why not fill me in on how your friends are doing now? That is, if you need someone to talk to that is not involved. Or at least not involved in your group."

Neither of them spoke for a moment. Both Bruce and Judith contemplating precisely what he meant by that, but then Judith said, "Yes. I would like someone to listen to me who is involved enough to know what I am talking about, but who doesn't care. Whoa, I don't think I meant it exactly how that came out."

Bruce laughed, "It's okay. I know what you meant. Tell me what's happening in Spring Falls."

For the next thirty minutes, Judith filled Bruce in. April and Ron were the first things on her mind. She gave him a brief history of how April and Ron had met and why April had walked out on him and come to Spring Falls.

And then how April had completely changed her appearance and fell in love with Cindy's art gallery. And how the two women who worked there had taken to her as if she was their mother. All that in just one day, all because of Paul's letter. So maybe it was a good thing?

After Bruce answered with a short, "Could be," Judith continued with the story. She had taken April to dinner at her favorite restaurant to celebrate, but then right after dinner, Ron showed up at her door and did what she thought was impossible—apologized to April right in front of her.

Bruce heard the doubt in her voice.

"So you aren't sure whether to believe him?" he asked.

"I guess not. I am not a fan of husbands that keep their wives contained, and that's what it has felt like to me all these years. But she loves him, and she believes him."

Bruce tried to imagine Judith contained in any way, and although he had just met her, he was positive that it would not be possible, and for a moment, wondered if anyone had ever tried.

"So what's next with them? Is April going back with Ron?"

"It seems not. April told him she wanted to stay in town for a while. He huffed off looking like thunder but then called later and said he would find a place for them to live in town so that they could be together."

"Not a fan of this solution?"

"No. I'm not, but I don't know why. I guess that's why I am angry. I don't know why."

"I barely know you, Judith," Bruce said, "but can I say that you are not in charge of all of this turning out the way you think it should?"

Silence again. Bruce waited, biting his lip while watching a bee moving from flower to flower on the tree.

"Will you always tell me like it is, Bruce?" Judith finally said.

"I'll do my best," was his answer. "Now, tell me about the other women."

As Judith relayed the latest—how Grace had gone back to Doveland, that Cindy and Marsha were on their way to Spring Falls, and that Bree had gone off on her own.

Bruce listened and wondered if Paul had meant to give him a gift too, or if this was just one of those things.

Either way, he decided not to be so angry at himself for taking the case or at Paul for coming to him. He'd take it as a gift instead. Because if he thought that way, perhaps it would turn out to be so.

Forty-Six

Bree didn't go far. In fact, she only went two blocks away and then, seeing a parking space, pulled in, turned off the car, and leaned back. She didn't know where she was going, only that she knew she had to go. She had to drive somewhere. But where?

For the first time in her life, she had no pre-planned path to follow. Yes, she would return to Spring Falls, at least to keep her promise, but it didn't mean she would return to live there. She and Paul had left for a reason, and she wasn't sure she could go back now, even though it was almost thirty years later.

Bree had always known what she wanted to do with her life and how to do it. Although life hadn't been exactly how she thought it would turn out, it had been close enough to what she had planned. She and Paul had decided to build a life together. He would do the work he loved, and she would write books. That had happened. And now that was over. At least the Paul part. She wasn't sure about the writing. She could stop and do something else.

Paul's life insurance and pension would take care of her for life, just as he planned. Besides, she had her own money. So what did she want? Who was she without Paul and her plans?

Maybe my plan is not to plan, at least for a few days, Bree thought. The idea made her feel a little giddy. No plans? On purpose? The idea was intoxicating. So drive, but where? Closing her eyes, she waited for inspiration to strike.

And then she heard Paul's voice in her head telling her to go where they had planned to go before he got sick. She knew exactly where he meant, but could she go there without him? Or would it be too painful?

Then she remembered what Grace had said, to live life for both her and Paul. Taking out her phone, she made a call. Yes, they had an opening, a last-minute cancellation. It was a sign. She would go.

Putting the destination on her phone, Bree smiled to herself. Yes, she was going back the way she and Cindy had come, but this time, on her own, and this time, she would let life lead her instead of death.

In Spring Falls, Ron was looking at houses, something he never thought he would do. It hadn't been in his plans for their life. He had moved April away from Spring Falls because he wanted a life that was only theirs. Now he would have to do something he thought he had prevented for good. He would have to share April with others.

Ron knew April didn't see it that way. She saw it as making a new life for themselves. They were childless now. They would have time to get to know each other again.

"People to hang out with," she had said.

"I have people to hang out with," Ron said. "I have work."

"But I don't," April said. "And I want that now."

They were in Judith's living room, being as quiet as possible. Although Judith had assured them she couldn't hear anything once she was in her bedroom with the TV on, Ron didn't put it past her to be listening in. Still, he knew it didn't matter. April would tell her what they discussed anyway. And no matter how hard he tried to get April to come with him back to the motel room he rented, she had refused.

Refused! He still couldn't believe it. His wife, who had always done what he asked, had refused? She was right. It was a whole new world. He resisted hitting the steering wheel of the car in his frustration. She was his wife. She couldn't refuse. But she did.

"I need to know you are serious about a new life first," April had said. "I want one and I want you to be part of it."

His "what about my work?" complaint didn't make a dent in her resolve.

"You travel a lot for it anyway," April said. "Make arrangements for the other times. Or quit. Or stay in Silver Lake and visit me when you can."

Ron's head almost exploded when April said those words, but he kept himself calm. It was what happened back at the house that had brought them to this place, that had made her choose Judith and the blasted Ruby Sisters over him.

He had to win her back. So Ron had smiled and said that he would do as she asked. He'd figure out work. He'd get a house for them and support her in the decision to do something else with her life.

"Just don't leave me," he begged. And he meant it.

And that was why he was looking at houses. To rent. April wanted to buy something, but he didn't want to wait for that. He wanted her back in his arms and his home again as soon as possible. They would keep their home in Silver Lake. Instead of traveling from there, he'd travel from Spring Falls, and their home in Silver Lake would be one of his stops.

Although he didn't like the idea of April getting too independent, a part of him realized that her independence would also mean his. She would be less worried about where he was going and when he'd be home. And when he was home, she would be all his. And when he wasn't home, he'd know exactly where she was. She'd be happy. He would be happy for her. That would work.

April said she wanted to live in town so she could walk to the gallery, because yes, she intended to work there. Maybe even take a few art classes at the community college.

Even though it freaked him out to think about her doing all these things without him, the reminder that they had met at the community college made him smile.

"I fell in love with you the minute you turned and looked at me, April. And I love you more each year. So yes, I'll do whatever you want me to do so you will be happy."

She had smiled back at him, her warm brown eyes sparkling, and said, "Thank you," and then snuggled into his arms as they sat together on the couch.

His little wren was returning to the nest. Now he just had to find the perfect place for them, and all would be well.

Forty-Seven

B ree took the same road back that she and Cindy had taken.
Route 86 was a beautiful drive, and she knew she had missed
a lot of it the first time worrying about what they would find in
Pittsfield. Now, she was not looking for anything, just enjoying the
beauty of the drive, and letting her mind drift away. Sometimes she
played music. Other times, she just let the silence take over.

She stopped along the way. Once for a bathroom break, once for
gas, and two times only to get out of the car to breathe and look at
the sky. How long had it been since she had done something just
to enjoy it? It was the road trip with Paul, she realized. They had
no plan other than to enjoy each other and what they found. Now,
doing this tiny trip without him was bittersweet, but lovely in its
own way.

The sun was setting behind her as she turned towards the
Athenaeum Hotel. She checked in quickly and then stepped out
onto the front porch and watched the last of the rays glinting off
Chautauqua Lake, glittering just beyond the long green lawn that
stretched out before her. She had made it—by herself.

It was the perfect place to collect herself before settling into a new life. *Thousands of people must have done the same thing here,* Bree thought. Built in 1881, the hotel was part of a long legacy of learning about new ideas and enjoying the beauty of nature and the music, writing, and art that it inspired.

It was why coming to Chautauqua had been on the list of things they would do together. She had wanted to come to one of the writing workshops they offered and learn something new. She would have come as a student, not as a successful writer. No one would have known who she was since she would have used her real name and not her pen name to register.

Even then, she had thought she wanted something different. But they never made it, and she never started a new way of life. A life where she was not hiding behind her writing. Probably because they both knew she couldn't do that. Well, she knew that, and Paul was her constant support in the life they had built for themselves, just the two of them.

So here she was. Ready to start that new life. Or was she? Was she still trapped in the decision she had made that meant they had to leave Spring Falls? If she returned there, would she be able to forget what had happened and what she had done?

This is not helping, Bree said to herself. *Forget the questions. Just relax.*

Bree chose one of the rocking chairs on the porch and settled in, telling herself that there was nothing to do but listen to the birds, breathe in the air, and stare at the stars as they slowly came into view.

She breathed in and out slowly, practicing her yoga breathing. Even though it had been months since she had last practiced, she fell right into the peacefulness of it and let go.

It lasted for all of ten minutes. Or maybe it was the relaxing that started it. Bree's mind raced back to when she first met Paul and declared him to be her future husband, and traveled quickly through the years until the day she called the morgue.

She reviewed all the moments in between. Most of them were ordinary, which made them the best ones. Coffee together, walking, her writing all day while waiting for the sound of the garage door opening, knowing that he was home. Reviewing the day together, grocery shopping, planning new curtains for the windows. All of them were ordinary memories that had made up a life she had loved.

All gone. The moment Paul died, that life vanished. The details of selling the house and leaving were just the outcome of that vanished life. All she had left were a few suitcases and his ashes sitting in an urn in a box in the trunk. And memories. That she had.

And now she knew Paul a little better. Now she knew the secret he had kept all these years. It didn't seem like such a huge thing, and she wanted to ask him why he didn't tell her. How could it have been that bad? But she knew she was looking at it as someone who didn't live it. She didn't know what it felt to believe that your parents died because you were arguing with them.

Of course, nothing could have stopped that driver from driving straight into their car. The fault lay entirely with the drunk driver. But would you be able to tell yourself that when you were just fourteen? Probably not. She remembered being fourteen. It was a hard time, anyway. Neither a child nor an adult—trying to test boundaries and discover freedom.

It would have been terrible if you believed you caused your parents' deaths by doing that. Yes, she could see how he had thought it was something he had to keep to himself.

And then there was Noreen Ferguson. Or Nora Gray and her dead child. Either name, it was the same woman. Just as changing his name didn't change Paul, he was still the same person.

But to blame himself for running? He was in shock. Terrified. Confused. Seeing his parents that way, of course, he would have run. He probably forgot there was someone else in the car with him. Her heart broke for that boy, and she understood her husband a little better.

She understood how that tragedy helped explain why he was always nervous in a car if someone else was driving. And why he never, ever raised his voice in an argument. Now she realized it was a part of himself thinking that he might cause another tragedy by doing so.

Bree didn't realize how long she had been sitting in the rocking chair until one of the staff approached her and asked if she would like a blanket, and then, seeing the tears on Bree's face, asked if she was okay.

"I am, thank you. And thank you for the blanket, but I think it's time for me to get some sleep."

"Don't forget, we serve a wonderful breakfast in the morning."

Bree nodded her thanks, climbed the old stairs up into her room, and, leaving the lights off, took off her clothes and fell into bed, feeling the warmth and safety of the hotel surround her.

This is the perfect place to look at choices I made in my life, Bree thought as sleep closed in, sweeping her away into dreams that she only vaguely remembered in the morning.

But the wisp of the memory was enough to make her decide to search for what she had lost. Even if she couldn't find the answer, at least she would have tried. She was a coward then, she realized. But, like Paul when he made his decision, she was young when she made hers.

But she wasn't young anymore, and hopefully no longer as afraid. Either way, it was time.

Forty-Eight

"Who were you talking to?" April asked as she poured coffee into her cup and stirred in the Chaga mushroom powder. Judith had convinced her to try it, and even though it was weird, she liked it. April liked that Judith seemed to have all kinds of new ways of living. Many new ideas she would have never found out about if she hadn't come back to Spring Falls.

Of course, Judith shared some of her weird health things when they would talk on the phone, but mostly, she had just nodded and smiled and not tried any of them. April remembered her parents and how they drifted from one health idea to another and how she had tired of constantly changing how the family did things. She had decided she wanted more stability when she grew up.

Which Ron had definitely provided. With Ron, she knew what her life would be all the time. So while living with Ron, Judith and her mushrooms were too much like her old life with her parents. Because as much as she had loved her parents, she didn't want to be like them. Besides, she knew Ron wouldn't appreciate a different diet or her trying out new foods and exercises.

And now after just a few days at Judith's, April wondered if she had been avoiding life that way. Telling herself she was too old to try something new or do something differently. But being at the gallery yesterday had done something to her. Or maybe it was the driving away that had started it.

For the first time since she and Ron left Spring Falls together, she had gone someplace by herself. Was that normal? Would the eighteen-year-old April have believed she would become a woman who would choose to live a life that was planned for her by someone else?

April didn't realize that she had been staring at her coffee and not moving until Judith asked, "April, are you okay?"

"Hum. Yes, just thinking. Kinda wondering how I became this person."

"Do you like the person you became?"

"Yes, and no. But things are changing now, aren't they?"

"I'd say so. Just think about it. You told Ron you wanted to stay here, and he agreed."

"He did, didn't he?" April said, smiling. "Who knew I had that in me? So, going back to my original question, who were you talking to?"

"That attorney guy, Bruce. I was trying to worm more information out of him."

"Did it work?" April asked, smiling to herself. It didn't feel as if that was the complete truth about why Judith called Bruce. But Judith probably didn't realize it yet, and it wasn't her place to tell her. Besides, there were too many other things to deal with than that now. Maybe that's why Judith didn't want to notice.

"Not really, but he implied that there was more to come."

"You mean, you think that it's not just about Paul changing his name or his wanting the Ruby Sisters to help Bree?"

"Well, definitely he wanted that. But maybe there's more."

April nodded in agreement, knowing that if anyone could figure it out, it would be Judith.

"Any news when the girls will be here?"

"Cindy and Marsha will be here tonight."

Judith didn't need to add that she had no idea when Bree would arrive. They had to wait and give her time to work out what she wanted to do. Although she dearly hoped that Bree would decide to move back to Spring Falls, because it would be wonderful to have all the Ruby Sisters back together in one place.

There would be so many things they could do together. For one thing, they could help plan Mary's baby shower. Mary had waited on them at dinner, impressing April the same way she had impressed her.

April had mentioned how wonderful it was for her to have met three lovely young women in one day and how much they had inspired her to look at her life differently.

"This was a perfect day," April had said. "A new look, a new life, and new possibilities with Ron."

Yes, Judith thought. *It had been a good day.*

She wasn't sure if the possibilities with Ron were exactly what April would get, but she was willing to give him a chance to prove himself.

People change, she told herself. *They learn what they have done wrong and correct it all the time.*

After all, that's what her business was all about—finding mistakes people make in their business and helping them correct them. Most of the time, their mistakes were accidental and unintentional. Only rarely did she find someone who intentionally did wrong in their business. And if they weren't willing to fix it and stop doing it, she always did something about it.

Sometimes what she did was more drastic than others, but she never liked to let people get away with anything that hurt other people, and that went double for the people she loved and protected, like her Ruby Sisters.

Judith hoped Bree knew when she came back to Spring Falls, not only was she the one who would protect her but was also the person who would figure out why she and Paul had not only left but stayed away, hidden. What could have happened that made them make that choice?

Whatever it was, Judith knew it was time to fix it, and she figured Bruce either knew what it was or had the way to find out.

She smiled to herself as she drove to the office. It felt as if she had found someone she could talk to and who listened and didn't judge her. She wondered what Bruce's story was. Perhaps that was what she should do today—a little searching for why Paul had picked Bruce as the keeper and distributor of his secrets.

Now, that sounds like an excellent way to start the day, she thought. *And I'll come home early and bake something for the girls.*

Yes, it was going to be a good day. April was at the gallery, safe and sound, with Mimi, Janet, and Mittens. Cindy and Marsha were together, and Bree, well, she knew where she was, and that was going to have to be good enough for now.

Forty-Nine

As promised, breakfast was delicious, and Bree took her time, eating it out on the patio where she could see the lake and say hello to the other guests as they walked by her table.

What a fantastic feeling, Bree thought, to be someone no one knows, and to be somewhere she had never been before.

All the world was open to her. She could choose to be anyone or anything. That's what it felt like anyway, and she let the feeling build until she could feel a little well of joy bubbling inside of her. Yes, the grief was still there, but the joy was there too.

For the first time since Paul had died, she felt free. And while she sipped her coffee, Bree realized she didn't have to think through her decision anymore. She had decided. It was time to see what else Paul had done. The thing she asked him to do, but never tell her what happened. He had kept his promise, and now she was going to break her promise to herself.

Because she realized that when he knew he was dying, Paul had decided to set her free. He couldn't make her do what she needed to do. He had to let her decide for herself, which was why he sent her on the trip and reunited her with her friends.

Yes, Bree said to herself, *I knew there was more to the last gift idea.* She just hadn't wanted to accept it. How could she? It would change everything.

She'd have to tell people. What would they say? What would these strangers sitting next to her say if she told them? That's when it finally hit her. They wouldn't care, they might understand, they might not, they might help her, they might condemn her, but what did it matter?

What about her? Was she ready to find out and do something about what she had asked Paul to do for her? Was she willing to fix it now? That was the only question that mattered.

And now that she had decided that yes, she was ready, she was afraid. But she was also excited. But, first, she needed to get back into some kind of self-care because she would need it. She had noticed that there was going to be a taiji class near the lake that morning. She'd join that, then maybe take a brief run—more walk than run—around the town. After that, she'd settle down with her computer and start the search.

But first, she had ideas. Not ideas about the search, ideas about a story. It wasn't fully formed yet, but she knew how it worked for her. She'd dream something, or someone would say something, or a tree would speak, or even a rock, and then there was an idea.

Usually, she did not know where the idea would take her, but she knew she had to write it down quickly because otherwise, like a butterfly, it would move on to the next person, and the idea would be lost to her.

So she scribbled a few things down in the tiny notebook she kept in her purse for those ideas, trying to make sure that she could read it later, and then headed to her room to change clothes.

She expected she would get more inspiration while doing something other than worrying, so she tucked a slip of paper and pen into the side pocket of her go-walk pants that worked for all kinds of exercise and headed to the lake. But not before applying sunscreen and grabbing her favorite baseball hat.

Self-care, she told herself, *begins here.*

By the time the morning was over, Bree was hot, sweaty, full of ideas, and hungry. All of which she took as a good sign. So far, the day had been perfect, and she could start the search after lunch. After all, she had waited twenty-eight years to do this. One or two more hours wouldn't make a difference.

But it wasn't just a few hours. Bree napped after lunch, sat on the porch again people watching, said hello to strangers, and let the afternoon drift away. Once Bree checked her phone and saw that Cindy and Marsha were almost home. But that was the extent of her paying attention to her past life.

Her life with Paul, her life in Spring Falls—Bree decided to put it all aside for one more day. She'd get started in the morning. Bree knew that a deep fear of what she would find was driving her actions, delaying her, increasing her resistance.

But since she had declared it to be a self-care day, that was what she would do. Tomorrow was soon enough to find out—because she wasn't just afraid for herself. Bree was afraid for everyone involved. Paul was safe. He was dead. But what about the living who did not know that she had a secret that would change not only her life but theirs forever? Maybe she had no right to do this.

The surety she had felt that morning had vanished and was sinking, just like the sun was sinking below the horizon.

"But the sun comes up in the morning," she swore she heard Paul say. Of course, he was always that way, reminding her that the next day would happen and it was up to them to enjoy it. So it was probably an echo of what he always said, probably stuck in her head forever.

So she answered him, the way she often answered him, "Sure, Paul, but it doesn't mean it will be sunny." And his answer had always been, "I disagree, my love. The sun is always shining."

If she didn't stop him, Paul would go into detail about anything and everything, so she would stop him before he went on and on about the sun and clouds and the other side of the world. She stopped him tonight, too. She didn't want to hear about shining suns. Bree just wanted one more night before the world shifted for her again. It didn't seem too much to ask.

Fifty

The morning in the art gallery sped by. Janet and Mimi were happy to help April learn how the gallery ran, and Judith stopped by before lunch to explain Cindy's bookkeeping and how to access the website.

It was only her second day at the gallery, but April loved everything they taught her. Besides, knowing she could help Cindy when she returned made it even more exciting, although she was a tad nervous.

Would Cindy be happy that April wanted to be part of her business? Judith, Mimi, and Janet assured April that Cindy would be delighted. Nevertheless, she couldn't wait until Cindy told her so herself.

Watching Mittens greet customers, April noticed how Mittens always seemed to know which ones wanted her to be part of their gallery experience and which ones were happy to have Mittens stay out of their way. It was a skill she wanted to learn.

After her bookkeeping lesson, the four of them sat down to have lunch together, and when Mittens chose April's lap to curl up in, everyone laughed and said that Mittens had decided that April was part of the gallery now. That made Mittens purr even louder in agreement.

Cindy always closed the shop for lunch, saying her customers understood or they didn't. But she got to choose how she ran her life. At least that's what Judith told her as Mimi flipped the sign over to 'closed' and put up the sign that said, "We'll be back at noon."

Janet had ordered pizza, and they were eating in the back room when April asked Mimi and Janet if they knew Mary Patterson who worked at ParaTi, saying that she had met her the night before and thought they might like each other if they weren't already friends.

"Sure," Mimi said. "We met her last year when she waited on us. You're right. We hit it off immediately."

"And now," Janet added. "We're in a writers' group together."

Judith put her pizza down and stared at the two women. "Writer's group?"

"Well, I'm in a writer's group with Mary, but Mimi tags along sometimes. She's more like my proofreader."

"So you aren't visual artists?" April asked.

"Oh, heck no," Janet answered. "We love the art here, and we love Cindy and this gallery. Cindy pays us well and takes good care of us, but I want to write books. Well, I do write books. Hence the writer's group."

"And Mary writes books, too?" April asked.

"Yep," Mimi said, taking another bite of pizza and then stopped seeing the look that Judith was giving her.

"What?"

Judith shook her head. "I just realized that I never asked you what you do, and then April comes along and asks the simplest question, and I learn something I would never have guessed."

"Well, aren't you about finding out what is wrong and then standing up for what is right?" April said. "Perhaps there was nothing wrong here that caught your eye."

"Sure," Judith said, trying to make light of it, but the whole idea that all of that was going on with these three young women and she was clueless, bothered her.

"You know what would be cool," April said to Mimi and Janet. "When our friend Bree gets here, perhaps she can help the writer's group."

"You mean the woman that is part of your Ruby Sisters group?" Janet asked.

Seeing April and Judith exchange glances, she added, "Well, we know that much anyway. Cindy told us what was happening before she left. She also told us a little about how you all have known each other since you were kids and why it was important to go help your friend."

"Which is totally brilliant, by the way," Mimi added. "But why would your friend be able to help the writers' group?"

Judith leaned back in her chair, looking at the women in the room with her as if she had never seen them before. Perhaps she hadn't. Maybe she was too short-sighted. Something was happening here that meant something. She knew it, but what?

"Because Bree is the writer R.B. Curtis."

Janet dropped her pizza and stared at April. "Say what? She's my idol. Oh my god, that's the woman coming here? That's your friend? Wait until we tell Mary and the rest of the group. This is epic."

Mimi smiled at Janet with a look that Judith had never seen before. *No*, Judith said to herself, *I've just never noticed it before. How blind am I anyway?*

There was a knock on the door, and Mimi peeked into the gallery to see who it was.

"Some guy is outside. Can't he read the sign?"

April looked at Judith and looked out into the gallery, and sighed. "Not some guy. That's my husband. And no, he probably won't care about the sign."

"Well, it's almost noon, anyway. Why not let him in? That way, we can meet him, and he can see where you work now."

April smiled. She liked the sound of those words. Yes, she worked here. So when she opened the door for Ron, he assumed she was smiling at him, and he scooped her up in his arms and twirled her around.

"Put me down, Ron," she whispered, trying not to be embarrassed. He did what she asked, but only because he had an audience and an announcement to make.

"I got us a house, babe!"

Mimi and Janet clapped, happy for their new friend. Judith stared, wishing she were pleased about Ron being there. She'd learn to like him for April. She'd done harder things. Perhaps she just didn't know him well enough to like or not like him. She'd find time to get to know him, and that would make the difference.

"Great," April said, trying to ignore the fact that she didn't feel as excited about that as she thought she would. She'd get there in time.

"Let me show you around where I work now."

There you go, she said to herself. *I told Ron. I told him that this is my new life, and he will be happy about it. I just know it.*

Fifty-One

No self-care today, Bree told herself. At least not the kind she had done yesterday.

Besides, she was so sore she could barely move. What was she thinking doing all that at one time? She needed to pace herself better until she was back in shape.

Instead, today, her self-care would be mental and emotional. She would find the information that Paul had kept hidden from her. Not because he was cruel, but because she had asked him never to tell her.

However, she was ready now, and she had to assume he had kept records so that she could find the information if she ever looked. Or at least left a hint for her, a thread she could pull to find the answers she needed.

She had Paul's laptop with her, and he had left her all the codes she would need to get into it. She even had a file box of Paul's papers in the car's trunk, just in case he had kept the information off his computer.

Where she would find the information was a mystery, but she was finally ready to look.

So after a lovely breakfast, a quick walk down to the lake and back, Bree returned to her room and plugged in Paul's computer.

It didn't take long for her to realize that she had more immediate things to deal with than looking for what he had kept hidden from her.

She had thought that giving away his clothes—except for the one shirt he always wore, carefully packed away in her suitcase, hoping his scent would never leave it—was the end of dealing with the logistics of his death.

But once she opened his computer, she realized Paul was still getting email. Mainly spam, but there were legitimate emails from people who apparently didn't know he had passed away. So she spent the morning writing to those people and fielding their responses, which only brought back the hurt and pain she had managed to contain. Luckily, Paul had no social media presence, so she didn't have to deal with shutting those channels down, too.

But by the time she had finished with the emails, she was mentally and emotionally exhausted, and Bree wasn't sure she could continue. Or that she wanted to. It would be easier to go back to Spring Falls and never tell a soul. She'd keep their secret forever.

But then she heard Paul's voice in her head. Not actually in her head, but there anyway, because it would be what he would say if he were physically with her now.

"Remember who you are looking for, Bree."

And that broke the dam. Until now, Bree had fooled herself into thinking that she was only looking for information. Impersonal information. But now she had to face that she wasn't looking for information.

She was looking for a person. Someone she had never met. She didn't know her name, where she lived, or who or what she loved.

She knew nothing. It was how she had wanted it to be and what Paul had done for her, because that was what she wanted.

And now, she didn't. Now she wanted to meet her. She wanted to know her daughter. And she could only hope that her daughter would want to meet her too.

But by the end of the day, Bree realized she had been living in a fairytale land. Paul had left nothing behind about her daughter. There were no clues. There was no information about the adoption agency he had used. Nothing. Not a shred of evidence that she had ever had a child. He had buried it all somewhere.

It was as if the nine agonizing months of bearing the child that she was too afraid to love, because of the violence of its conception, too embarrassed to tell anyone what had happened, as if it had been her fault, had never happened.

But it had. And Paul had agreed that they could move away and tell no one if that was what she wanted.

"But is it necessary?" he had asked. "It's your child. I'll love it as if it was mine. No one will know."

"Can't. Won't," Bree had said over and over again. She had reasons. Good reasons. Maybe the child would look like the man who attacked her. Then people would know. Every time she looked at it, she would relive the memory.

"No," she would cry in Paul's arms. "I can't do it. I can't make this baby live a life where I would have to decide to love it every time I saw it. It's not fair. Whoever this person is going to be will be better off without me."

Paul had not agreed with her, but he had agreed to do what she wanted. He had also agreed with her decision to never return to Spring Falls—to stay away from the Ruby Sisters because they would figure it out if they saw her.

They had to make a clean break. Make a new life. Just the two of them. She had promised him they would have children of their own one day. But something had gone wrong at her daughter's birth, and it had turned out that she was the only baby Bree would ever have.

Both of them pretended it was okay, and in some ways, it had been. They never spoke of the child again. She had never held the baby. They had whisked it off to the adopted parents waiting in the wings. She didn't know who they were. She had not wanted to know. The only reason she knew it was a girl was because she heard two nurses whispering about it.

She never asked Paul what adoption agency he used. He only told her it was done.

And now that she wanted to know, there was nothing to find. She had been wrong twenty-eight years before, and she was wrong now. Paul had not wanted her to find the child. His gift was as simple as it appeared. Get a new life, and return to the Ruby Sisters. It was over. His gift was over. That would have to be enough.

But now, she wasn't sure it would be. The only choice that remained was what to do next. And at that moment, she didn't want to do anything. She was done. All of it was over.

Fifty-Two

T hey're here!" April yelped as she ran out the door.
    Judith followed, feeling as if her heart would burst with
happiness, but trying not to let it show too much. She'd let April
be the expressive one.

Except there was no getting around the squealing and hugging
and crying going on, and finally Judith let herself go and joined in,
smiling so hard she thought her face would crack in half. And then
April started crying so hard no one was sure if she was happy or sad
until she said, "I'm so happy. I haven't seen you all for so long."

Judith waved at the neighbors, who couldn't help but see and
hear what was happening on her front lawn. The woman across
the street was smiling, her hand on her heart. It was hard to miss
the joy that the four of them were experiencing.

"Let's go inside," Judith said, ushering the three women inside
and into the living room.

Once they had all seated themselves, Judith said, "Tell us
everything."

Marsha looked at Cindy, who nodded at her to go on, and she
told an abbreviated version of their trip and what they found in

Pittsfield. Of course, they had texted some of the information to Judith as it was happening, but Marsha filled in some details, so they had a fuller picture.

"So that was Paul's big secret? That's sad. We would have all understood," April said. "But he gave us a last gift, didn't he? After all, here we are all together again."

"Almost," Cindy said. "There's Bree. Without her, it's not the same. I wanted to stay with her, but she insisted on having some time to herself, which is probably a good thing. But she's been by herself all these years, so I don't understand why she needs more."

"She's always liked more alone time. And she wasn't totally alone before. She had Paul, after all. They were together, and now she's alone differently and needs time to process it. Despite that, I worry. Do you think she will be okay?" April asked.

Checking her phone, Judith said, "Well, she's still at the lake. Let's send her a picture of us together, which might inspire her to come home soon."

"That's a great idea," Cindy said. "But could Marsha and I get cleaned up first? Perhaps we can meet for dinner and have someone there take a picture?"

They made plans to meet at ParaTi in an hour. In the meantime, Judith texted Bree that they were going to dinner and would send her a picture of the four of them later.

There was no response. Judith tried not to worry. Bree could be sleeping or maybe taking advantage of the beauty of Chautauqua. She'd been there once for a lecture series and loved every minute of it. She hoped that was happening for Bree, too.

An hour later, the four of them were seated at a table Judith had reserved for them. As Judith had hoped, Mary was working that night, and when she came to their table, Judith introduced her to Cindy and Marsha.

"I heard that your friend that isn't here yet is the writer, R.B. Curtis?" Mary said as she brought their drinks. "Mimi and Janet shared that information with the writer's group. I hope that's okay. We agreed not to tell anyone else until we get her permission. Sometimes people who write using a pen name don't want people to know."

"Thank you, Mary. I didn't think about that when I blurted the information out. Bree might not want people to know. Would you make sure no one tells until she says it's okay?" April asked.

"No problem. I'll text the group right now to remind them that it's our secret. But still, we are all excited to meet her. Besides, she's your friend. She must be amazing."

"She is," Cindy said. "Without Bree, we wouldn't be in this group. She's the one who brought us all together and kept us together throughout school."

No one needed to add that she had left them, and it hadn't been the same since then. The group had drifted apart. Each of them played a role in their group, and Bree was the leader even if she hadn't acted that way for a long time, and maybe that was not what she wanted to be anymore.

"And here you are again," Mary said. "Now all you need is your Bree."

As the four Ruby Sisters ate, they filled the time with reminiscing, lots of giggling, and a few tears. After it was over, Mary took the picture, and Judith sent it to Bree, saying they couldn't wait for her to be there, and then the group would be complete.

When there was still no response, Judith said, "She's probably not near her phone." Everyone agreed, even though each of them worried privately.

Cindy felt like getting in her car and driving back to Chautauqua to find her. But she was tired and would never make it. In the morning, perhaps.

Back at the cars, they hugged again and promised to meet in the morning for coffee.

"And then I'll see you at your gallery," April said to Cindy. "I hope it's okay that I am working there. I mean, not actually working there, but being there and helping."

"It is the best thing ever," Cindy said. "And we'll figure out a real salary for you because I can't think of anything more wonderful than to have you part of what we do there."

"And then there is Mittens," Judith said.

"Oh, I bet Mittens loves you," Cindy said.

"Well, I love her back."

It took another round of hugs and "I will see you in the morning" calls before everyone finally got into their cars—April with Judith and Cindy with Marsha. Marsha had left her car at Cindy's house so they could come to dinner together.

As they drove home, Marsha said, "Thank you for letting me stay with you until I have a place of my own."

"I love having April in the gallery and you in my house. Stay as long as you want. It will be fun to brainstorm what you want to do next because I assume you are going to want to do something."

"Something," Marsha agreed. "Not sure what that is yet, but having a place to stay will make it easier to decide. Will Bree stay with Judith and April?"

"Well, you know Bree. Doubtful. She'll want to live alone. Besides, April won't be at Judith's long."

"Why not?"

"Ron found them a house to rent, and once he gets it fixed up, April will move there. Although she says, he will be gone a lot. I guess he was gone a lot in Silver Lake, too. So, mostly she will be on her own."

"Oh. That's good," Marsha said.

Marsha knew Cindy would assume that she thought it was good that Ron was coming to be with April. But what she meant was that it was good that Ron would be gone a lot.

Marsha didn't think she would ever be comfortable around Ron. But she would do it for April because that's what friends did.

Fifty-Three

Bree hid her phone in the desk drawer, not being able to stand seeing it. Judith's texts were driving her crazy. First, the text that everyone had arrived safely. That was good to know, even though she didn't respond. But then the pictures, and more notes, until she couldn't stand it anymore. Couldn't they just leave her alone?

That's when she tossed her phone into the drawer, but being practical, she took it out, plugged it in, and then put it back. She knew she would eventually have to face everyone, starting with herself, but she couldn't do it now.

All night she tossed and turned, alternately hating herself and being angry with both herself and Paul, and then forgiving him, but never herself.

How could she have been so stupid? Or cruel? she asked herself. Was it kind to let her child go?

Maybe she was just a selfish woman who didn't want a child. Just because her baby resulted from a violent act didn't mean she wouldn't turn out to be an amazing woman. And now, thanks to Paul being such a master of secrets and then dying on her, she would never, ever, know.

After a night of restless sleep, she had breakfast sent to her room, unable to face anyone or anything. Only after that, and a long shower, and then a brisk walk around town, did her head begin to clear, and she realized she would solve nothing by remaining by herself and wishing things were different.

She had lived with her decision all these years, and hating herself for taking so long to realize it was the wrong one would not make it better.

But it was Cindy's text that finally broke the spell.

"Get here, or we are coming to get you."

Bree couldn't help but laugh and, knowing that was precisely what would happen, texted back that she was leaving and would be there in a few hours.

"Counting it down. Starting now," was Cindy's reply. And then a flurry of texts followed with emoticons of all kinds, and that's when she realized it was a group text.

Yes, I am part of this group, Bree said to herself. *There's no escaping it.*

She would have to put her regrets aside and begin a new life, and with their help, she could do it. Besides, she had a book idea that kept niggling at the back of her head, and she realized she was ready to write again.

Maybe not what she wrote before. Perhaps even write a new series under her own name. She'd call her agent when she got to Spring Falls and talk to her about the idea.

Still, Bree knew she would never get over what she had done. She'd just have to live with it. She had lost her daughter forever, and that was just a fact of life—just as Paul had died and would never be coming back.

But Bree realized that the only way she could begin a new life was to tell her friends what she had done. So before leaving, she asked the group if they could meet at Judith's. She wanted to explain why she had left before, because it was what Paul would want her to do.

They all agreed to meet at Judith's, and Judith asked if she wanted to stay with her or did she want a room at a hotel in town.

Before answering, Bree closed her eyes, imagining herself at Judith's or by herself at the hotel, and realized she had to choose a hotel and hoped Judith would understand. Judith's response of a thumbs up reminded her that they all knew her well. At least the part she had shared, and now they'd know her big secret. Or at least the important part. That she had a daughter and gave her away. That was all that was important to tell.

A few hours later, she pulled up to Judith's house and took a deep breath. To begin a new life, she would have to face the past.

"Some lady called while you were gone," Mimi said to Cindy as soon as she walked in the door.

Cindy was emotionally exhausted. They had met at Judith's, and Bree had told them the story about her daughter. They had all cried, hugged, and assured her it didn't mean they loved her less, which Bree seemed to believe.

At first, they tried to get Bree to tell them the actual circumstances of how she had a daughter, but she refused, saying they didn't need to know. Cindy disagreed. It was still keeping a secret, and it worried her, thinking that the only reason Bree refused to tell them was it would affect them somehow. But at least part of Bree's secret had been released, and that had to be a good thing.

However, hearing that some lady called and needed her to call her back did not make Cindy happy. All she wanted to do was go home, hide in her room, and go to bed. Marsha had already gone back to the house, and Cindy suspected that she, too, was done for the day.

Bree was at the hotel. Judith had gone to her office, and April had stayed at Judith's. She had only come back to the gallery to check in. The trip had worn her out more than she realized. Mimi and Janet had done an excellent job of keeping the business going while she was away, but she couldn't keep asking so much of them and wanted to let them know she'd be back full time in the morning.

So when Cindy learned some stranger had called and needed to talk to her, there was no way she wanted to deal with it at that moment. Seeing her exhaustion, Mimi apologized and said she tried to get the woman to tell her what she wanted, but she refused. Said she could only talk to Cindy. She had something to say about her next-door neighbor, Noreen Ferguson.

Fifty-Four

T he package from the neighbor arrived a few days later, but
instead of opening it by herself, Cindy suggested they get
together at her house for lunch the next day.

Bree had stopped by the gallery to say hello the day before,
looking thinner than ever, and seeing Cindy's worried face said she
was doing okay. She reminded Cindy that they had all agreed to
give her time to heal, her way.

However, that didn't stop Cindy from worrying. She and Judith
had met that morning at the coffeehouse, the way they used to
before Paul's letter arrived. They tried to pretend that everything
was back to normal, but they both knew it wasn't.

It was Judith who finally said that she was worried about the
package.

"Maybe it's nothing," Cindy said.

"Well, why the secrecy? Why not just tell us what's in it?"
Judith responded, thinking about her conversation with Bruce
that morning. She had called him to tell him about the package,
and after a long pause, he had asked her to call him back after they
opened it.

"Why can't you just tell me everything, Bruce," she said, not expecting him to but wishing the whole secrecy thing was over. Although Bree told them she was moving on, something still didn't feel right. She just couldn't put her finger on what it was.

A few hours later, everyone arrived at Cindy's for the lunch that Marsha had prepared. The package lay on the dining room table, and while they ate and chattered about the weather, they all tried to pretend that it wasn't there.

Finally, Bree put her sandwich down, having taken only a few bites, and said, "Please, just open it. It's probably nothing anyway, but I can't stand it anymore."

Everyone laughed, and Judith gave the package to Bree to open. Bree opened it slowly, hoping against hope that it was something that would ease the pain that she felt and was doing her best to hide from her friends.

A note from the neighbor lay on top explaining that the rental's owner had arrived earlier than expected and found these papers and pictures when cleaning out the house. She had stopped him from throwing them in the trash. She had told him she knew someone who might want them.

"Maybe they will help Paul's wife, somehow," the note said.

"What does this mean?" Bree asked, looking up from the box. She put a small stack of pictures and a folder on the table.

Judith took the stack of pictures and spread them out. "It looks like she had a daughter?"

"So cute," Marsha said, picking up a picture of a little girl with long, dark hair and brown eyes.

"How could she have a daughter?" Bree whispered.

"Oh," Judith said.

"Oh, what?" April asked.

"Maybe that's what he meant."

"Who?"

"Paul. It's something Grace said. She called a few days ago and said she remembered something Paul had said the last time she saw him. Of course, he was only fourteen at the time, so she hadn't thought much of it."

"What did he say for god's sake?" Marsha said.

"As Grace remembered it, he said something like 'I'll make it up to her somehow someday.'"

"No!" Bree whispered. "He couldn't have. Could he?"

Marsha stared at the picture in her hand, thinking that the little girl did look like Bree.

There was a long pause while everyone thought about what Grace had told Judith.

"I think that he may have, Bree," Judith said. "It makes sense. He felt responsible for Nora's baby's death, and then you had a daughter. It probably fit together for him. Like some divine plan."

"And would explain why there is nothing in these papers to tell you who this child was," April added, having spent the last few minutes looking through the folder.

"This folder is just old bills and notes to herself. Nothing else. Not even letters or references to her daughter. Nora must have been afraid that you'd find out someday and come take her child away."

"And why she changed her name!" April added.

All the women sighed in unison, thinking of what they had found. Was it good news or bad news?

"So now I'll never find my daughter?" Bree asked, looking at each of her friends.

Cindy reached over to hold her hand. "We will, Bree. This is better than before when you had no idea what had happened. Now, we know that Paul probably gave your daughter to Nora. His lawyer might know more. We can track her down now that we

261

have her picture. And if Nora had your daughter all these years, you know she was safe and loved."

"Yes!" Judith added. "We'll find her, Bree. I'll call Bruce. Maybe he has more information. In fact, I am sure he does. He's been so secretive. And we'll have you do one of those DNA things, and perhaps we'll find her that way."

"Promise?" Bree said.

"Promise," Judith answered, and everyone else nodded.

But all of them knew it was a shot in the dark. Nora had been careful. Paul had been thorough. All that they could hope was that Paul had led them all to this, with good intentions, wanting Bree to know that her daughter had been safe all along.

But that didn't mean that they would find her.

Fifty-Five

W eeks went by. The flowering trees dropped their petals, and roses bloomed. The Ruby Sisters' days had settled into a new routine. Their being together differed from when they were young and from each of their lives before Paul's letters had arrived. Nothing had stayed the same. But they were together, and they all agreed it was a version of life that was becoming better each day.

The best part, Judith told herself, *is no one felt on edge anymore.* At least that's what they told each other when they got together. They agreed they learned all there was to learn, and all they could do was move on.

Maybe Bree's DNA would find a match. If not, then perhaps someday it would happen. Bree said she was good with that, but the strain on her face often said otherwise.

When Judith had called Bruce after they opened the package, he sighed, saying he was glad to be done with it. He would mail the last piece of information that Paul had given him. Paul had asked him to send it only after Bree discovered he had given the child to Nora.

They had gathered together the day that Bree opened that package, too. She had said they didn't need to be there, but the rest of the Ruby Sisters disagreed.

In the package that Bruce sent, Bree found another letter from Paul. In the letter, Paul said what they discovered was true. He had given Bree's daughter to Nora. It helped him feel as if he had made something right that had been wrong. Paul said he prayed Bree would agree that he had done the right thing.

The package also contained the agreement he had made with Nora. It was not a legal agreement. There had been no formal adoption. Technically, Bree was still this child's mother. But since they didn't know who the child was, it didn't help. In fact, for Bree, it made it worse. Although Paul apologized and said he hoped she would understand, Bree didn't understand, and she didn't think she ever would.

Bruce told Judith he was sorry. He knew only what Paul had told him. He and Paul had argued about it, and he had told Paul that he needed to tell Bree if he knew more.

But Paul refused. He said it was his last gift to Bree. "Leaving her not knowing is not a gift, Paul," Bruce had said. It hadn't made a difference.

So when Bruce and Judith talked, he asked her if she thought Paul had believed Bree would enjoy the search.

"Maybe. His gift brought us all together again. And she knows her daughter was loved and cared for all her life. However, I think he was wrong, not telling her more, because Bree took the DNA test and then stopped looking. She claims it doesn't matter. That she is moving on.

"But it clears up the mystery of where the money went that Paul was taking out of their accounts. It went to Nora and Bree's child. I supposed if Bree would have noticed, Paul might have told her then. But she didn't, so he didn't."

Bruce said, yes, Paul had mentioned that to him. If she would have asked, he would have confessed.

"Which means he knew where Nora and the child were the whole time?"

"Looks that way, doesn't it?" Bruce replied.

"Well, why didn't he tell her in the package where she is?"

"I think he wanted her to want it enough to keep looking."

"But she's not. If the DNA doesn't show any answers, she's not doing anything else. Bree has given up looking," Judith answered, frustrated with the dead Paul and even with Bruce because she still thought he knew more and was just not saying.

Bree might have stopped looking, but Judith didn't. She thought it should have been easier now. They knew who had raised Bree's daughter, which meant they should have been able to find her school records or track down people that knew Nora and her daughter. But there was nothing. And although she knew money left their account, there was no trail to where it had gone.

"Nora must have changed her name while her daughter was growing up," Judith finally said to Bruce after another fruitless search.

"And then moved back to Pittsfield that last year of her life." Bruce agreed. "Did she want to be found then?"

Although Judith wanted to think that Nora had gone to extreme measures to ensure no one would ever find the girl, she understood. Nora was probably concerned that Bree would change her mind and want her daughter back one day. And since there was no legal agreement, Bree would win.

But then, after all that time, why did Nora keep it a secret so long after it didn't matter anymore?

Bruce said that obviously it still mattered to Nora. She wanted her daughter never to know. Probably for the same reason Paul had kept his part of the secret. She felt guilty.

Still, it didn't sit right with Judith. The world shouldn't work that way. Love shouldn't keep people apart. But in this case, it did, and she didn't like it one bit. It was something she wanted to fix, but she didn't know how to do it.

So life went on. Judith helped Bree find a house to rent. Bree wasn't ready to buy yet, but she had agreed to stay in Spring Falls, which made everyone happy.

Marsha was still living at Cindy's, trying to figure out if she wanted to open a dance school in Spring Falls or not. It was a chance to begin again, but what kind of beginning did she want? Maybe something completely different, Marsha thought. But what that would look like remained elusive.

April was still living with Judith, saying she was waiting for the house to be ready. She had told Ron she didn't want to rent the house he had found. She wanted to buy a house.

Everyone knew she was stalling, including Ron. But he said he understood. He would court her all over again. However, he still had his work, so he was gone most of the time, leaving April to deal with finding a house.

When the Ruby Sisters met for coffee or lunch, if they brought up Paul's letter, it was to say thank you to him for bringing them all together again.

Truly, Cindy thought, *it was a gift worth giving.*

No one mentioned that there was still a missing piece for Bree. But she told everyone she was starting a new book series and was caught up in that world, so she was okay with not knowing.

No one truly believed her, but they let it be.

Fifty-Six

Once Cindy heard about the writer's group, she offered the gallery space as a place for them to meet. Mimi and Janet helped her turn one of the back storage rooms into a cozy retreat space for them.

To celebrate the opening of their new writer's space, they invited the Ruby Sisters to come to a meeting to see what it was all about and to thank Cindy for providing the space for them.

Bree had declined. The other four said yes. Although they weren't interested in becoming writers, they wanted to see what a writer's group did.

Janet introduced the four of them to the other two writers. A mother of five who decided to try her hand at writing children's stories and a young man working on writing fantasy.

Janet explained to the four Ruby Sisters that every writer's group was different, and even theirs was never the same. She reminded them that Mimi wasn't a writer herself, but she was an excellent critic and sounding board. And they were hoping to have Bree come one day and give them some pointers and insight into the business of writing.

"But," Mimi said, "We understand she is still mourning her husband."

"And her daughter," Janet added. "And when we heard that she took a DNA test to find her, it inspired all of us to do the same."

"But not because you are looking for your parents?" April said. "You know who they are, don't you?"

"Well, most of us do," Mary answered. "But of course, you know I don't. I never really cared before, but now that I am pregnant, I thought I would do it, just in case I could find my parents. They might want to know they are going to be having a grandchild. And medically, it would be good for me to know too, just in case."

"And Janet wanted to know too," Mimi added.

"Janet, were you adopted too?" Cindy asked in surprise.

"Well, I don't think of it often. But when Mary and I got to know each other, we realized we had similar stories. We were both raised by our mothers and neither of us knows anything about our birth father.

"And, surprisingly, we both moved around all the time. More times than we can count. My mom didn't change my name as much as Mary's did though."

Seeing the astonished looks on the Ruby Sister's faces, Janet laughed. "I know, weird, right? How did we both end up in the same place with the same story? And to add weirdness to weirdness, our mothers died, so the answers to all our questions died with them.

"A few years ago, when my mother was alive, I begged her to tell me about where I came from, but she refused, and I never could find the adoption papers.

"For a while, I decided it didn't matter. I'm a grown woman now. But Mimi and I are thinking about having a child, and we could adopt one or do the sperm donor thing. If we go that route, I want to know more about my parents."

"The things you find out at writer's groups," April said. "And you and Mary kinda look alike. Except for the hair!" Marsha added.

Janet laughed. "We do, don't we? Just another one of those weird things to add to the mix."

"So you all took the test?" Cindy asked,

"Yep," Mary answered. "We all agreed to do it together. Besides, when we heard about Bree looking for her daughter, it reminded Janet and me that perhaps we have family looking for us."

The Ruby Sisters looked at each other, and they knew they were all wondering the same thing. How likely was it that these two women were looking for their mothers while Bree was looking for her daughter?

"Weirder things have happened," April whispered. The four of them giggled and then turned back to the group, listening as they shared their writing, looking at the two adopted women and wondering if it was at all possible that one of them was the woman Bree was looking for.

Then they laughed. That only happened in books.

Fifty-Seven

The Ruby Sisters decided to throw Bree a surprise birthday party at the gallery. Cindy, April, and Marsha were designing the party, and Judith was in charge of getting Bree there.

Bree had become more and more of a recluse, saying she was writing, but everyone was worried anyway. When they did see her, she barely spoke. For the rest of the Ruby Sisters, it felt as if their founder and leader had still not returned. Her body had, but not her mind and spirit.

Cindy asked Mimi, Janet, and Mary to help with the party, too. With Marsha and April's help, they made origami birds and blew up balloons. Once the gallery closed for the day, they spent the next few hours putting up all the decorations and turning the gallery into what Mimi said was a magical fairyland.

When Mary brought out the ladder to hang the disco ball, Marsha stopped her, saying no ladder climbing for her. Mary had protested, but everyone agreed with Marsha. Now that it was obvious Mary was pregnant, there would be no more ladder climbing for her until after the baby arrived.

Mary had smiled and said thank you and then left the room. Cindy watched her go and then followed her. She found Mary quietly sobbing in the storage room.

"What's wrong, honey?" Cindy asked and then waited until Mary had wiped her eyes and blew her nose.

"Did I mess up my make-up?" Mary asked.

"Just a bit, but we can fix it. Do you want to tell me what's wrong? Or do you want me to stay out of it?"

"It's not a big deal, really. It's just everyone is so lovely to me, and I wish I could share it with my mom."

"I'm sorry," Cindy said. "It must be hard. Is there anything we can do to make it better?"

Mary pulled her phone out of her purse. "I got the DNA results in my email today, but I am afraid to look. Do you think we could do it before the party?"

"Of course. Just us?"

Mary smiled. "No. How about I look at it out there with everyone else? Maybe Mimi and Janet got theirs, too, and we could all do it together?"

Cindy looked at her watch. They had plenty of time before Judith would arrive with the unsuspecting Bree.

"I really, really don't want to go out tonight, Judith," Bree said again.

She was angry about the whole thing. Judith kept pushing her to get out of the house, and she didn't want to. But no matter what she said, Judith wouldn't listen.

"I am not taking no for an answer, Bree," Judith said, using what they all called 'the voice.' It always worked, and she hoped it would work this time.

She had arrived at Bree's apartment, and Bree had reluctantly let her in. She had invited Bree out for dinner a few days ago to celebrate her birthday. Bree had said no. There would be no celebration.

Judith had protested. "We haven't had a chance to celebrate together for almost thirty years, so please, do it for me."

"Just you?" Bree had asked.

Judith crossed her fingers and said, "Yes, just me. We'll go somewhere private. We'll not even talk about birthdays. Maybe you could tell me about the book you are writing?"

It had been that last sentence that had hooked Bree. Sometimes it did help to talk about what she was writing. Paul had been her sounding board before, so she had thought that perhaps Judith could fill that role, at least once. It was worth a try.

But now that the time had come, she didn't want to go. She didn't enjoy going out at night. She liked being alone, and she didn't want to change her clothes or put on her makeup. So by the time Judith arrived, she was sure she could convince Judith to leave. She had tried to call her, but Judith had ignored both the calls and the texts she sent trying to call it off.

Now, standing in her house, Judith was an immovable force. And then she used the voice, and Bree knew there would be no getting out of her agreement.

"Okay, but no birthday talk. Just a quiet dinner, you and me. And not long either. I go to bed early so I can write in the morning."

Judith winced inside and, crossing her fingers again behind her purse, agreed. "Now go change."

"Why?" Bree asked, suspicion in her voice.

"Bree, no matter where we go, someone will see you. Is this what you want people to see?"

Bree looked down at her sweatpants and old t-shirt and sighed. She knew her hair was a mess, too.

"See, this is why I don't want to go," Bree whined. "It's too hard."

"It is not. Go get ready, and do it fast. I'm hungry, and you know how I am when I am hungry!"

Bree tried not to laugh, knowing it would break her bitter mood, and she didn't think she wanted to give it up just yet. But she couldn't help it.

Too many memories of a hungry Judith surfaced, and she started to laugh, and then Judith started to laugh, and Bree's lousy mood vanished, just as she feared it would.

Thank god, Judith said to herself after Bree left the room to change. It would have been hard to bring that bitter person to a celebration. Judith took out her phone and texted Cindy that they would be a tad late.

Cindy texted back that they were in the middle of something and having extra time would be good.

Middle of what? Judith texted.

When there was no answer, she wondered what could be so important she didn't get a response.

Hurry up, Bree, she said to herself.

Was it something good that was happening? If so, she wanted to be part of it. If it wasn't good, was it something she would have to fix? Either way, she needed to get to the surprise party as fast as possible.

"Ready yet?" she yelled down the hall to Bree, who, like Cindy, chose to ignore her.

Fifty-Eight

While they waited for Bree, they gathered in the small writer's room. The main lights in the gallery were off so that Bree wouldn't suspect anything.

When Judith texted they were running late and would let them know once they had left the house, Cindy said they had time to do what Mary wanted to do and look at her DNA results with all of them present for her.

"Did you get yours yet?" Mary asked Mimi and Janet.

"We downloaded the app, we just haven't looked yet," Janet replied. "I'm a little afraid to look."

"Me too. I didn't want to be alone when I looked."

"Do the three of you want to do that now?" Cindy asked.

"Please," the three of them said together.

Mimi knew her parents, so she wasn't expecting any surprises, so she looked first. Most of her family hadn't done the test yet, so she saw a few distant cousins. It surprised her to learn how many nationalities made up her genetic base.

Maybe everyone should have to do this, Mimi thought to herself. *Then people would have to stop putting people into different races and see we are all one.*

"Your turn," Mimi said to Mary.

"Why not Janet first?"

"I think it's you, Mary," Cindy said. "Your baby is waiting to know, too."

Mary reached down, took out the necklace that had been hiding below her sweater, and kissed it.

"For good luck!" she explained when she saw everyone looking. "My mom gave it to me. I used to wear it all the time to remind myself that I was still the same person even though mom kept moving us around and changing our names. So it was a reminder that we were the same people no matter what name we used.

"I haven't worn it for a while because now that I feel settled and at home here in Spring Falls with my husband, I didn't need a necklace to remind me.

"All I had to do was look around and see my friends and home, and now this wee one reminds me every time she kicks. But I thought I would wear it tonight to bring my mom along with me."

"Wait," Mimi squealed. "You know it's a girl?"

Mary giggled. "Not officially. It just feels that way."

It was Janet who noticed that the three Ruby Sisters had gone silent and were exchanging looks.

"What's up with you three?"

Cindy took a deep breath and asked, "Where did you say you got that necklace?"

"My mom. Why?"

"And why did you move all the time and change your name?"

"Wait, what's going on?" Mary asked, the color draining out of her face.

"Well, it is weird you did that," Janet said. "I know we did the same thing, but I always thought it was weird. Sure, people often move a lot, as we did, but they rarely change their name every time."

Mary hesitated, feeling as if something terrible had happened, and now she was going to find out why.

"I guess. I asked mom once, and she said she liked change. She made it fun, even though I was not fond of it all that much. When right before she died she told me she had adopted me, I wanted to ask her all kinds of questions. I tried, but she kept saying it was best not to know, and I went with that."

"But you have the results of your DNA in your hand, so you must want to know now," Janet said.

"Sure. It seems important that my baby knows where she comes from, just in case..." Mary trailed off, looking at the Ruby Sisters. "You know something, don't you?" she asked. "The three of you know something, and you are afraid to tell me. What is it!"

"Well, we don't know anything for sure. But we know someone who used to have a necklace just like that," Cindy said.

"And seriously, girlfriend," Mimi said, "That moving around thing is weird. Are you sure you weren't hiding from someone?"

"Oh, god," Mary said, turning pale. "We were hiding from someone. How did I not see that?"

At that moment, Cindy's phone pinged. *What timing,* she thought. *Saved by the bell.*

"Listen, Mary. Everything is okay, but Bree is on her way, and she's had such a hard time. Could we wait and do all of this afterward? I promise, Mary, we will be here for you as you work this out."

Mary stood, trying to hold herself steady despite feeling like her legs had just been kicked out from underneath her.

"Of course. Why not? Besides, I don't think I want to see the answer right now. But I need to freshen up just a bit, if you don't mind."

When Cindy moved to come with her, she said, "Don't worry. I'm okay. Just need a moment."

Marsha stood and asked, "Mary, could I see your necklace? I want to check something on my computer. Maybe it only looks familiar because of the design. It will just take a moment, and I'll give it right back to you."

Mary nodded, and April stepped behind her and unclasped the necklace, handing it to Marsha. When Mary walked out of the room, the three Ruby Sisters sighed as Marsha put the necklace into her pocket.

"What is that about?" Janet asked.

"You just don't want her to be wearing the necklace right now, do you?" Mimi said.

At that moment, they all heard Judith's car pull up and rushed to the gallery, waiting for the signal from Judith.

"Why are we here?" They heard Bree ask Judith as they stood outside the gallery door.

"Sorry. Cindy left me some papers, and it would be easier for me to pick them up now so I can work on them the first thing in the morning."

Judith turned the key in the lock and flicked on the light switch, illuminating the magic fairyland the six women had created.

"Oh," Bree breathed. "It's beautiful."

"Surprise!" Cindy, April, Marsha, Mimi, and Janet said. "Happy Birthday!"

"You are so bad!" Bree said, hugging Judith. "But this is beautiful. Thank you."

Seeing Mary walk into the room, Bree turned to her and said, "You look beautiful, Mary! Pregnancy agrees with you."

Mary hugged Bree as she said, "Thank you," and then stepped back and looked at Marsha.

"Why is she wearing my necklace?"

Crap, Cindy thought. *Of all nights to wear that, Bree.*

Bree's hand went to her throat. "Your necklace? Do you have one like this? My husband gave me this."

Marsha reached into her pocket and handed Mary her necklace. "And her mother gave her this one."

Judith took one look at the scene and realized what everyone was thinking. Standing together, Bree and Mary looked almost alike. How had they not seen that before? Was it possible?

"Well," Cindy said, taking over. "This has the makings of an unforgettable birthday party. Perhaps we should open your DNA app now in this magical room, Mary. Shall we?"

"Did you get your DNA results yet, Bree?" Cindy asked.

"Yes. Afraid to open it, though."

"Well, now is the time. You first, though, Mary."

"Can't. My hands are shaking too hard."

"Let me," Judith said, taking the phone and looking at the results.

Her voice catching, she said, "Well, it turns out, Mary, that you have found your mother. Her name is Rhoberta Curtis."

"Can't be," Bree breathed in.

"And yet it is," Judith said.

"Wait, you know who she is?" Mary asked, looking at Bree and Judith.

Cindy and April had begun to cry, and Mary felt as if all the blood had gone to her head, thinking that it was true. Something terrible had happened.

Mimi and Janet stood to the side, holding hands, knowing they were watching something happen that should be impossible.

"What's happening?" Mary whispered.

Judith walked to Mary, took her hand, and then reached out and pulled Bree close to her. She could feel Bree trembling as tears gathered and overflowed.

"Mary, meet Rhoberta Curtis. Otherwise known as Bree Mann or R.B. Curtis. Our Bree. Your mother."

Fifty-Nine

*I*t's a good thing that the waiting room in the hospital is big, not comfortable, but big, Judith thought, looking around at all the people waiting for Mary's baby to be born.

It hadn't taken long for Mary and Bree to bond. Although Mary said she was beyond grateful for finding her birth mother, she couldn't call her mom. Nora had been—and had to remain—her mom.

Bree had agreed without hesitation and suggested that Mary could either call her Bree or whatever she was going to have her baby call her.

Grandmother names were tossed around for the next few months until Mimi suggested the Swahili word for grandmother, Bibi.

"Close to Bree," she said, and everyone laughed and agreed.

Now Bibi, or Bree, was in the delivery room with her daughter Mary along with Mary's husband, Seth.

After the miracle of finding her daughter, Bree told the Ruby Sisters that she could barely contain her happiness at being part of something she had never let herself imagine for herself. The birth of a grandchild.

Both Mary and Seth wanted to wait to find out the baby's sex, although Mary kept saying she knew it was a girl. If it was, they knew what she would call her, but they wanted to wait before telling anyone.

In the waiting room, Janet and Mimi sat together holding hands, perhaps thinking that someday it would be them waiting for their baby.

April and Ron also held hands. Judith thought they were probably remembering the birth of their children.

Marsha was pacing, her nervous energy making everyone just a little uncomfortable, But that was Marsha.

Cindy kept herself busy, making sure everyone had what they needed. She had closed the art gallery for the day, a sign on the window explaining that a friend was having a baby. It was a small town. She knew they would understand.

One side of the waiting room had windows that looked out onto a stand of trees, and Judith let herself imagine how many joyous moments the trees must have witnessed.

Their leaves were almost gone, only the oak tree holding onto its copper leaves. The maple's red and yellow leaves were in the process of being stripped off their branches by the wind that was howling outside.

Marsha said the trees were dancing, and everyone laughed and said, of course you would see them that way.

Four months had gone by since the night that Bree and Mary realized who they were to each other. It was a night no one there would ever forget. First, there were tears, hugs, then a brief explanation and apology from Bree to Mary about what she had done.

Mary kept telling her that wasn't important. Nora had been a wonderful, caring mother to her, and there was never a moment that she didn't feel loved by her.

"I think if she were still alive, she would be happy to know you, Bree," Mary had said.

Bree hoped that could be true. And since then, she had talked to Nora every night and thanked her for taking such good care of Mary and raising her to be such a lovely young woman.

She didn't know if Nora could hear her, but she hoped being grateful would help heal her own heart and ease the guilt that still crept up and caught her when she was least aware.

"How are you doing?" Bruce asked, handing Judith the coffee she had asked for.

Judith smiled and thought again what a handsome man he was and how kind he was to be there with them all. He had arrived the day before, after she told him it could be any day now.

"It's a great excuse to take off for a few days," Bruce had told Judith. "It's been years since I did anything like this, and it shocked my secretary when I told her."

Secretly, Judith was shocked too. But if Bruce wanted to make the trip, she was happy he was coming. Surprisingly happy, but she kept that to herself. After months of talking on the phone, it was the first time they had met in person.

She had picked Bruce up from the airport and then taken him to the coffee shop where she and Cindy would meet before all of this had started.

After a few minutes of small talk, both of them doing their best to make it feel as if it was only two colleagues meeting in person for the first time, and nothing more, Judith asked, "Did you know Paul meant for Bree to find her daughter? He must have known that she was here in Spring Falls and that eventually we would all figure it out."

"I think that's true. I think Paul knew where Bree's daughter had gone. When he first talked to me, I suspected there was more to the story than he had given Bree's child to Nora. That seemed a little cruel to me, and I had not known Paul as a cruel man. And, of course, he knew there would be clues. Like the gravestone that said she was a mother, since he arranged to have it put there. And the necklace he gave to Nora like the one he gave to Bree. He must have known that sooner or later, Bree would see it."

"But why draw it out that way? Why not just tell her outright?"

"Well, if he did that, would you all have come together how you have? Don't you think his gift was not only the two of them reuniting, but all of you now living in the same town again?

"I think he knew that Bree would have to work through it all to get her 'mojo' back, so to speak."

Judith laughed at Bruce's description of what had happened to Bree, well, with all of them, after getting Paul's letter. They had all come out better for it. At least, for the moment.

Judith didn't let herself dwell on what was going on with April and Ron, who, although united in the waiting room, didn't seem to be united in everyday life.

But that was for another time and place. And nobody was going to upset Bree again by asking about Mary's father. All they knew was that it wasn't Paul.

Right now, it was about waiting for the newest addition to their Ruby Sister's family. Everything else was a mystery to be solved another time.

Sixty

"Bibi," Mary said, reaching up and clasping Bree's hand. "Isn't she beautiful?"

Bree nodded, tears streaming down her face, thinking it was the best day of her life. It had all started the moment she saw Paul and knew her life was with him. And although Paul was no longer present, his last gift to her was giving her back what she had lost.

"Thank you, Paul," she said to him, and for a moment, she thought she felt his hand on her back.

Then Seth placed Rhoberta Nora Patterson in her arms, and she finally felt as if she had come home.

Author's Notes

As I wrote *A Last Gift*, all the Ruby Sisters became so real to me I began a conversation one day about one of them with a friend, thinking I was talking about an actual person.

I've spent most of my life working with women: with my dance company, as a financial planner, as a coach, as a teacher, and guiding The Women's Council for many, many years.

Plus, I have two daughters, three granddaughters, women friends and have shared life's ups and downs with them. I pulled from all of that long life experience for the Ruby Sisters, which is probably why they are so real to me.

I can't wait to learn more about their lives in the following books in this series.

If you have read the *Stories From Doveland* novels, you have already met Grace. It was fun bringing her into this series to play a minor, but essential, part of Bree's story unfolding.

As for the road trip? My husband and I took one in 2000. We explored the country for almost a year, looking for a place to call home. The rest stop, the lake, the GPS stories are all from that trip.

And Pittsfield, too, was part of our road trip. It's close to where two dear friends, Dorothea and Linda, live, and they provided some background to help with that part of the story. Thank you!

I've been to Falling Waters more times than I can count, starting long before the official tours. If you ever have a chance to visit, go! It's incredible. Just thinking about it, I can feel its magic.

The Bree and Paul love-at-first-sight story came from my parents (although I have experienced it myself).

As I have heard it told, my parents told their friends they would marry the first time they saw each other. They married less than a month later and remained married for sixty-four years until my dad passed away. Although my mom says he is still around, and I am sure he is.

When I wanted to begin to write fiction, I went to a Chautauqua Lake writers' conference, where I was lucky enough to end up in Anthony Doerr's workshop. He, and the place, were the perfect way to begin this part of my writing life.

It's always fun naming characters. Sometimes I pick a name because it means what I want the character to represent. Or I change a character's name because I know I will have trouble saying it when I record the audiobook.

Other times, I have to wait until they tell me their name as I write. However, I named Mimi and Janet after my grandmother, named Janet Lewis, but we called her Mimi. It gives me a chance to think about her as I write about these two women.

And yes, I had a group of friends when I lived in San Diego in the eighties who would be asked to leave restaurants because we were laughing so hard. No, drink and drugs were not involved—just the joy of sharing.

I wish that for all of you, no matter your age or gender since we all want the same thing. To love and be loved.

In friendship, Beca

Learn more about *The Ruby Sisters* series at BecaLewis.com. Join my mailing list to be the first to know about new releases, or follow me at your favorite place to buy books.

Acknowledgments

I could never write a book without the help of my friends and my book community. Thank you, Jet Tucker, Jamie Lewis, Barbara Budan, and Diana Cormier for taking the time to do the final reader proof. You are a loyal and much-loved reader team. You can't imagine how much I appreciate it. And to Dorothea Green and Linda Morse for introducing me to the Berkshires and their background information on Pittsfield.

A huge thank you to Laura Moliter for her fantastic book editing.

Thank you to every other member of my Book Community who help me make so many decisions that help the book be the best book possible.

Thank you to all the people who tell me that they love to read these stories. Those random comments from friends and strangers are more valuable than gold.

And as always, thank you to my beloved husband, Del, for being my daily sounding board, for putting up with all my questions, my constant need to want to make things better, and for being the love of my life, in more than just this one lifetime.

Connect with me online:

Facebook: https://www.facebook.com/becalewiscreative
Instagram: https://instagram.com/becalewis
TikTok: https://tiktok.com/@becalewis
Twitter: http://twitter.com/becalewis
LinkedIn: https://linkedin.com/in/becalewis
Youtube: https://www.youtube.com/c/becalewis

Also By Beca

The Ruby Sisters Series: Women's Lit, Friendship
A Last Gift, After All This Time, ...

Stories From Doveland: Magical Realism, Friendship
Karass, Pragma, Jatismar, Exousia, Stemma, Paragnosis,
In-Between, Missing, Out Of Nowhere

The Return To Erda Series: Fantasy
Shatterskin, Deadsweep, Abbadon, The Experiment

The Chronicles of Thamon: Fantasy
Banished, Betrayed, Discovered, Wren's Story

The Shift Series: Spiritual Self-Help
Living in Grace: The Shift to Spiritual Perception
The Daily Shift: Daily Lessons From Love To Money
The 4 Essential Questions: Choosing Spiritually Healthy Habits
The 28 Day Shift To Wealth: A Daily Prosperity Plan
The Intent Course: Say Yes To What Moves You

BECA LEWIS

Imagination Mastery: A Workbook For Shifting Your Reality
Right Thinking: A Thoughtful System for Healing
Perception Mastery: Seven Steps To Lasting Change
Blooming Your Life: How To Experience Consistent Happiness

Perception Parables: Very short stories
Love's Silent Sweet Secret: A Fable About Love
Golden Chains And Silver Cords: A Fable About Letting Go

Advice:
A Woman's ABC's of Life: Lessons in Love, Life, and Career from
Those Who Learned The Hard Way

About Beca

Beca writes books she hopes will change people's perceptions of themselves and the world, and open possibilities to things and ideas that are waiting to be seen and experienced.

At sixteen, Beca founded her own dance studio. Later, she received a Master's Degree in Dance in Choreography from UCLA and founded the Harbinger Dance Theatre, a multimedia dance company, while continuing to run her dance school.

After graduating—to better support her three children—Beca switched to the sales field, where she worked as an employee and independent contractor to many industries, excelling in each while perfecting and teaching her Shift® system, and writing books.

She joined the financial industry in 1983 and became an Associate Vice President of Investments at a major stock brokerage firm, and was a licensed Certified Financial Planner for over twenty years.

This diversity, along with a variety of life challenges, helped fuel the desire to share what she's learned by writing and speaking, hoping it will make a difference in other people's lives.

BECA LEWIS

Beca grew up in State College, PA, with the dream of becoming a dancer and then a writer. She carried that dream forward as she fulfilled a childhood wish by moving to Southern California in 1968. Beca told her family she would never move back to the cold.

After living there for thirty-one years, she met her husband Delbert Lee Piper, Sr., at a retreat in Virginia, and everything changed. They decided to find a place they could call their own, which sent them off traveling around the United States. They lived and worked in a few different places before returning to live in the cold once again near Del's family in a small town in Northeast Ohio, not too far from State College.

When not working and teaching together, they love to visit and play with their combined family of eight children and five grandchildren, read, study, do yoga or taiji, feed birds, and work in their garden.

CPSIA information can be obtained
at www.ICGtesting.com
Printed in the USA
BVHW032328010722
641126BV00012B/268